# Counterpart

Rorie Smith

TAN TAN BOOKS

Produced by simonthescribe

Published 2014 by Tan Tan Books, Freathy, Cornwall.

tantanbooks.co.uk

ISBN-13: 978-0-9929503-0-9

Printed and bound by CPI Group (UK) Ltd, Croydon, CR0 4YY

To you both

"A chaque être plusieurs autres vies me semblaient dues."
(To every being, I felt, several *other* lives seemed due).

Arthur Rimbaud
A Season in Hell

# 1

There is a photograph I took in Ireland a long time ago. It is of a man in the bar of the Milford Hotel in Milford, County Donegal.

The man is dressed in dark suit with white shirt and open collar. He is in a corner seat. He is talking, pointing with his glass. The bar is lit by a pale shaft of mid morning light and outside the rain falls steadily. It is essentially a black and white scene. But my focus, the photograph is being taken with available light and a wide angle lens is on his socks, which are bright yellow.

This is the exception. The picture that only works in colour.

I photographed mainly in black and white in those days, developing the pictures myself and selling them to the newspapers and magazines.

But it was not possible to live off the small amount these publications paid. So I wrote all sorts of articles as well.

But in front of me now, here in my small house in Cornwall (at the moment I divide my time between Cornwall and Northern Ireland) is the best photograph I have ever taken.

I spent days searching for it. In the end I found it in a drawer in the bedroom under a pile of clothes. I recognised it from the back by its frame. Now it is dusted it off and sitting on the desk in front of me.

It breaks my heart to see how beautiful Supin was in those early days. This is before England, before Plymouth, before Parkinson's disease. Her face is so delicate as to be barely real.

But an examination of the print shows a lack of sharpness in the tones. I should get another print done.

In fact the longer I study the picture, the less satisfied I become with it. There are other pictures where I have got the ratios just right. Three to one between sky and sea. Figures positioned slightly off centre to left or right. If I had cropped this picture an inch in to the left, it would have made all the difference.

A lot of people don't realise how mathematical it is. The positioning of the figures has to be exact.

The white washed cottage called Hilltop on Ballyman Road forms the backdrop. It overlooks the sea at Bray. Supin is to left of centre behind the line of roses which make up the foreground. She is dressed in plain Thai sarong and her hair is simply styled around her face. The horizontal lines of the trellis work on the front of the cottage lead the eye into the centre of the picture.

I hadn't noticed that before. The curtains on the ground floor window are closed. So it is still early morning. She has been walking bare foot in the damp grass. The early morning sun shining on her delicate young face.

Actually I have taken better pictures. I once took a picture of the EEC Commissioner for Fisheries, a certain Mr Finn Olav Gundelach. He was at a conference in Gweedore going face to face with the Irish fisheries minister Brian Lenihan. This picture ended up, via a photo agency, on the front page of the Irish Times.

But what makes this picture perfect, despite the flaws in its composition, is that it was taken with love.

We went back there thirty years later but the house had been pulled down and Supin did not get out of the car because it was raining.

But it was that summer that we set off on our tour of the west of Ireland in the old Triumph Herald. This was a car that had previously belonged to Ida, my great aunt. Years later it was given to a certain gentleman, who I am not going to name, who left it dirty and dishevelled in a builder's yard. But to me it was always an elegant little car. I recall on the inside the beautiful walnut fascia dashboard. On the morning we set off Supin carefully washed and polished the whole of the outside.

The reason for the tour was that I had got a commission from a newspaper. I was to write a report on the state of the fishing industry. But I was not operating under any sort of mandate. No changes of government policy would be made because of my findings. The report would simply do to fill several pages of the newspaper.

We started in County Donegal because that was where my mother and the Bluffer were living at the time. We combined business with a family visit.

At the court house in Letterkenny we listened as judgement was pronounced on the skipper of a Spanish boat that had fished over quota. Afterwards I interviewed the skipper via the court interpreter. Then we went to Killybegs where I spoke to Joey Murrin, chairman of the Irish Fishermen's Organisation. After that we visited Arranmore, going up and down in a small boat.

Then we travelled on down the west coast. We visited all the fishing ports, staying several days in Galway. We ate, we drank, we slept, we laughed. One day Supin put on a swim suit and we ran across the strand together plunging into the freezing water.

In the evenings we sat in bars and listened to fiddle players and sang rebel songs and got tiddly on Guinness. One night Supin, not realising how strong the beer was, fell over on her bottom and had to be lifted up by two brawny fishermen. That was the first and last time I ever saw her drunk.

Then one evening as we travelled south we heard a report on the radio that a man had escaped from jail. He was said to be hiding out on the bleak area of exposed rock called the Burren which we had passed that afternoon. The thought of the poor man out there by himself made us shiver.

When we got right down to the south we visited Baltimore and took a boat out to Sherkin Island. Then on Cape Clear Island we looked at a rundown house which was for sale for a thousand pounds.

When we got home Supin cooked in the kitchen and worked in the garden, it had got very overgrown. She must have heard the sound of the typewriter as I worked my way through my notes and wrote up my report.

At the beginning of the week I went into Dublin to the offices of the Sunday Independent newspaper on Middle Abbey Street.

In those days newspaper offices in Dublin had a very specific smell. It was the same smell, a sort of mixture of disinfectant and soot, that you used to get in railway stations and engineering works. I made my way to the top floor and handed in my report to a large man sitting behind a desk. Then at the end of the week I returned and went to the payment wicket on the second floor. There I peered through the gloomy bars and gave my name and was handed in return a brown paper envelope with the money for my articles.

I wrote all sorts of articles for the papers in those days.

There was an English man, I think he was from Liverpool, who worked for the Irish Press. He handed out the ideas for articles and he was always concerned about what he called ' value for money.'

At Easter, on his instruction, we bought a dozen different types of chocolate eggs and removed the packaging and weighed them. Supin carefully recorded the results in a notebook. Then we divided the price by the weight to work out which Easter Egg was the best value.

One morning a week later we were lying in bed when I turned on the radio to RTE and there was a man reviewing the main stories in the papers and the details of our researches were considered important enough to be included in the broadcast.

After that I took photographs of the unofficial horse races that were held by the tinkers on the streets in north Dublin.

There were other articles that were more serious. In a pub in Dolphin's Barn I met two armed robbers. It was at the time when armed robberies, it was all mixed up with the drugs trade, were getting out of control in the city. One of the men was called George Royal, I recall that. He was in the middle of telling me how they prepared for a bank robbery when he said suddenly, 'Well why don't you come out with us on a job?'

So I went to see a solicitor called Garrett Sheehan who in those days defended the armed robbers. I said if I sign an affidavit declaring that I am a journalist writing an article, and have nothing to do with the armed robbery itself, will that be a defense if we are stopped by the police? When he said no, of course not, I dropped the idea.

After that it was time to leave Dublin and come to England.

We loaded up the car, we had changed by then to a Ford Escort estate. In Ireland at that time you could drive on a provisional licence and Supin had gone all round the city in it without receiving any instruction.

We stopped when we came over a rise and could see Dartmoor ahead of us. We all got out and looked silently ahead. We were like the Joads staring at the promised land. The car was piled up to the top with children, clothes, even small bits of furniture. We all stood there for a moment looking at our future.

When we arrived in Plymouth and Supin had passed her test we bought a green and white Citroen 2CV. I have a recollection of her wearing a beret as she drove it. During that period she was always busy. She made jam and elderflower wine and took up carpentry.

I can see her outside the house one afternoon. She has bought a small palm tree from the garden centre and is planting it in the garden facing on to the road.

Then there is another memory of coming to the house one afternoon, it would have been about the same time. I am ringing the bell. I must have forgotten my key. She comes to the door in a sort of sailor's hat with a pencil behind her ear and a saw in her hand. She is building a kitchen cupboard and looks very happy.

I went past the house the other day and the palm tree is still there but now it is over the top of the roof.

Here is another picture. The greenhouse at the back of our garden. Black and white again. Supin planting out seeds, her face looking hot. She is absorbed in her task. It is easy to read too much into a picture. But is there the first shadow appearing? Has she had the first sense about the awful thing that is coming down the track to destroy her?

The first symptoms appeared two years before the diagnosis. One day Supin was walking along the pavement by the house and I noticed she was dragging her leg. A month later she was having difficulty holding her knife at the table.

## 2

My mother, bless you Mum, was a painter and my sister who was called Alison and who lived in Northern Ireland liked to plant trees.

The walls of my small house in Cornwall are covered with my mother's paintings and I study them frequently. They seem to me, I am not trained as an art expert, to fall into four categories. The first are amateur water colours as produced by English ladies of a certain class. The second category is much the same as the first, except that she seems to have concentrated more. The detail is more precise. There are a couple of still lifes that are rather touching. The third category are groups of thin stick like riders on horses that people who know about art have looked at and stopped and nodded and said, 'Do you know I think your mother had something there.' There have even been comparisons made with Raoul Dufy. In the fourth category I can only find three pictures and it is difficult to believe that they are by the same artist. They are mountain scenes in lurid acrylics and the brush strokes are angry and incisive. The effect is startling and they always catch the eye of visitors to the house.

There were four of us in our family. My mother, my father, known as the Bluffer, Alison and myself.

My sister Alison did many things in her life, all to her credit, including raising a fine family, but there are two things I would like to report on here. The first is the stoic and courageous way she dealt with the many illnesses that struck her. I picked up the phone one day, we were both in our thirties then, and was told that she would not be coming to lunch because she had suffered a stroke.

In the hospital she was lying on her side surrounded by tubes and drips. But when she came out I never heard a word of complaint and by her good humour and her strength of will she made a full recovery from the stroke.

But then she died thirty years later after suffering for ten years with all sorts of other illnesses.

It was in the last years of her life she took to planting trees. How many people express themselves by planting trees? By the end Alison had planted enough trees to constitute a small arboretum.

Every time I went to see her I had to stand with a stick in the field while she marched off to get the perspective, to make sure she was planting them in the correct place.

Sometimes she would disappear inside the house and up the stairs to her bedroom and look out of the window to see that everything was correctly positioned.

She spent the last weeks of her life in that room. She would have been able to look out of the window to see where the trees would grow. Was she thinking then, as the clock ticked away the final hours, she must have known it was nearly the end, of generations future?

By concentrating hard I can see the outline of a future face ( or is it still her face?) looking out of the bedroom window staring at the fully grown trees.

Then it occurs to me that she may have left a key, a code. Will the pattern of the trees eventually spell out a message?

Every time I go back there I walk by the trees and say hello to them and then report to my dear sister lying in the cemetery that they are growing nicely and that in a year or two they will do her proud.

# 3

I had known the Bluffer was a spy ever since I was a boy when I watched him descending into the garage with a brown envelope marked OHMS(*) to meet his Russian contact.

When he emerged again and if it was a Saturday we would go down to the Windmill on Whiteley Green in Adlington. My mother and Alison and I would sit in the car drinking Vimto and eating crisps while he went inside and drank beer.

I can name them all now, the men he drank with in the Windmill. They were all good honest men, rugby men, Manchester men, business men in the textile and other trades. As far as I am aware he was the only spy among them.

The only other person I remember clearly from those days is a workman who helped build our house and he was called Terry Tibbert. He was a drunk who was run over by a council lorry when it was reversing. It was after that, so the Bluffer said, that council lorries began to carry reversing bleepers. Terry Tibbert lived in a council house and used to keep a pig in the front room. So the Bluffer said. We used to call his wife Mrs Terry and she came in and cleaned for us. We voted Conservative were members of the AA and watched the BBC. They voted Labour and watched ITV. That is how the divide was in those days. Soon after my grandfather died, he was called Arthur Cropper, I remember hearing my mother on the phone talking to a friend saying, 'Well he was no spring chicken you know.' Well now my mother is gone. As is the Bluffer and Alison and Supin and Terry Tibbert.

After the war the Bluffer went up to Cambridge and studied Russian under Professor Elizabeth Hill before being sent to Germany to debrief Russian defectors. He said they used to communicate with each other by tapping on the pipes of their cells.

It was almost certainly in Germany that he started on the manuscript that was to become Counterpart.

This manuscript, along with the report from the private detective and all his other files, is in the old grey filing cabinet which is to the left of the desk in the house in Northern Ireland, where he spent the last years of his life. I am sitting at the desk now. From the window in front of me I can look out on to the vegetable garden where he used to dig when the weather was fine.

My mother left her paintings and my sister left her trees. Supin was a cook and a gardener. But for the Bluffer it was words. He seems to have written on every subject under the sun. In fact the filing cabinet is so stuffed with his files it is beginning to lurch dangerously to one side.

When he died, aged ninety two, he was still able to turn an argument on a sixpence. He was obdurate, cranky, bluff. Boy was he ever bluff.

Three weeks after the funeral The Daily Telegraph carried a long obituary. It was a Saturday and he was given the honour of sharing the page with Dietrich Fischer Diskau, the greatest baritone voice of the 20th century.

But what was never included in that obituary was a particular discovery he made. There are others who have reached similar conclusions but have then shied away from what they have found. The Bluffer confronted it all head on.

The Bluffer had worked out that there is an equal amount of light and dark in the world and that one cannot exist without the other.

He also had the bizarre idea, I think, that if he could somehow scoop up a small portion of this darkness he might be able to save a few people from the terrible misfortunes that would otherwise befall them. That, in my opinion, was a heroic gesture equal to all his war exploits.

Chris ( the Bluffer's mother) was tall and stern and smoked menthol cigarettes. She did the Daily Telegraph crossword puzzle and had been on the local council. They said she should have gone to university because she was clever. But the Bluffer was quite categoric in his denial of my assertion that my mother had been frightened of her. Perhaps I had posed the question wrongly. Though she was always kind to me, we were all certainly wary, cautious.

Harold, the Bluffer's father, is only a faint ghost like presence. An outline, a pencil sketch of a man, lying in a bed. He was in charge of the cigar department at W.D. and H.O. Wills in Bristol and kept bees and played cricket. The Bluffer said they called him Smiter because he could knock a cricket ball out of the ground. The strange thing is that I am probably the last person alive who still remembers him. They say that a person only really dies when there is no one left alive who remembers him. But when he died first, in the corporeal sense, the Bluffer says he found in his wallet a photograph of a woman that he did not recognise but that he did not tell anyone about it.

(*) OHMS. On Her Majesty's Service. The frank on an envelope usually indicative of a communication from the Inland Revenue.

# 4

Supin is already coming out of the hospital with the results of the scan when I arrive. She gets back into the car and settles herself and then hands me a slip of paper ripped out of a notebook and folded over. I open the note and see that Dr Gibson has scrawled two words, Parkinson's disease. The words are written diagonally over the page so that they cross the lines. For a moment everything goes blurred but then it clears and I look at her. There is no change in her expression. She is anxious to get on. For the moment the words, in English, mean nothing to her. They will do.

Later I am in the front room when I hear her answer the phone. She is telling the Bluffer that she has something called Parkinson's disease but that she has been told not to worry. I can sense the Bluffer's shocked reaction as well.

At the time of the diagnosis Supin is just forty six years old.

The morning of the funeral. Twenty five years after she is first diagnosed with Parkinson's disease. I have been dispatched into the town to buy flowers. Walking through the underpass I pass a man with a beard sitting on the ground. He is asking for change and looks miserable. Normally I would have given him a few pence but today I open my wallet and give him a note. He looks up, mumbles something and I reply that today is a special day for me. He looks at me oddly. He suspects a trap. He thinks I am religious. Then I say that after thirty one years of marriage I am going into town to buy flowers so I can bury my wife. At this he jumps to his feet, gives a firm salute and then advances forward and hugs me and neither of us can stop the tears from coming. All this is true.

They never give you the real story about Parkinson's disease. They waggle your bones, check your gait, talk about increments of pills and make further appointments for three months down the line.

When we pressed they only said that Parkinson's disease was a neurological malady with certain discombobulating effects. Certainly they never told us that it was also a rip snorting fire cracker that was going to zip zap through all our lives.

I pick up a pamphlet at the specialist neurological centre at Frenchay Hospital in Bristol where the surgeons ( bless you all, nurses too) are preparing to open up the top of Supin's head while she is still conscious and insert a series of electrical wires attached to a pacemaker that will give her an extra seven years of life. The pamphlet states that eight per cent of Parkinson's disease sufferers will develop gambling problems. This is because the drugs release inhibitions. Supin's father was a gambler. A lot of Thai people are gamblers. So a possibility has become a probability.

Even now I like gamblers. They have dared to place themselves outside society. They are not like drunks. They are not going to bore you to death or beat you up. I equate them with tramps and musicians and anyone else who can't hack it the normal way. They are not slackers, not idlers. They concentrate for hours over the tables making charts and studying form and consulting almanacs.

I should hate them. The Bluffer hates them. Shakes his head and screws up his eyes as if physically in pain. Something to do with his upbringing. All bicycles and rowing and sitting up straight at table. He says there was a system in the house where he grew up in Keynsham. Anything to go upstairs was placed on the bottom stair and the next person going up took it with them. The Bluffer never said if the same system operated for coming down but I assume it did. They had two weeks holiday a year in a guest house in Beer in Devon and swam every day whatever the weather.

Supin and I ran a restaurant called the Thai Coffee House on Sutton Harbour in Plymouth. I have pictures in front of me now of the opening. Supin is standing next to one of the Thai monks who have been invited to offer a blessing. She is in full Thai costume and looks very stiff and nervous. At that time, it was still many years before Phra Maha Laow opened the Thai Buddhavihara Temple in Kings Bromley in Staffordshire, the monks came from the Buddhapadipa temple in Wimbledon.

I put down my pen. In the strange film that is unspooling before my eyes I can recall the scene frame by frame.

It is now a month now since the diagnosis and Dr Gibson has put Supin on a medication called Sinemet. This replaces the dopamine that has been lost and is the first line of defence in the fight against Parkinson's disease. The dosage is low at first but is increased over the years. So the doors are slowly opening.

Supin gets up from where we are sitting.

A new man has come to work for us in the restaurant and he is a regular at the casino. We are new comers here, we have never gambled before.

She walks casually over to the Blackjack table to watch our new employee. He has his back to us.

Then very slowly he turns around and with a deadly sweet diabolic smile he shows her his hand and whoompphh ( as the Bluffer might say describing the sound of a particularly sweet piston engine) that is it, she is gone.

The main players in the adventure that followed are George Lynes, Ivor Dryer, Mr Chong, Jackie a head waiter at a Chinese restaurant, and our consultant neurologist Dr. Gibson. I have just looked him up on the internet and found that his first name is John. Almost everything that happened, and which I will recount, centred around Supin's bizarre decision to begin carrying a gun.

# 5

When the Bluffer died I spent two weeks at his house in Northern Ireland. I went through his papers and then arranged transport of furniture and my mother's pictures before returning the key to the landlord.

I got a valuer in but he said the only real worth was in the silver.

Then as I was going through a wardrobe I discovered a flat brown paper parcel tied up with string which had obviously not been opened in years. I opened it up on the dining room table and found that it contained a series of etchings. They seem to be a portfolio sold by an art dealer in Karlsruhe in 1900. I leaf slowly through them before checking on the internet. Then I sit back and look at them for a long time. I can see them now in the dealers, peering earnestly at the portfolio. The salesman is making his pitch. They are persuaded to buy and the portfolio is brought home. But who are they? And why are the etchings not framed and hung on walls? Why have they been left in their brown wrapping paper for me to find a century later?

I took them to a valuer who examined them closely. Then he checked against an art data base and whistled through his teeth and said you've done alright haven't you.

The Bluffer and my mother married during the war. Then after the war the Bluffer, who was from Bristol, moved North to join the clothing business run by his father in law Arthur Cropper.

Then twenty years later the Bluffer moved the base of the business to mid Wales and we bought Llugwy Hall on the banks of the River Dyfi for six thousand pounds.

There are times when I think I know the detail of the Bluffer's life better than my own.

It was later in their lives that the Bluffer and my mother moved to the Irish Republic and then on to Northern Ireland to be near my sister Alison.

When I first went inside Llugwy, it would have been 1967 when I was seventeen, there were geese in the hall and they had to pull down a whole wing because there was dry rot.

There was a fireplace big enough to roast an ox, a dozen bedrooms and woods and fishing, plus the usual leaking roofs and ancient plumbing. They rattled around in it very happily together. The lawns ran down to the river. In summer it was light and airy but in winter it could be dark and brooding.

I have been back three times since the Bluffer and my mother left.

The first time was to celebrate their fiftieth wedding anniversary. We were all there then, the Bluffer, my mother and Alison and Supin. I was standing on the lawn and the Bluffer opened a bedroom window and shouted out and it was like old times. We were all back together again. I remember Alison laughing so hard at dinner I thought she was going to cry.

The next time was when we scattered my mother's ashes. She died ten years before the Bluffer.

That was a sad day. The sky was grey, a thin rain was falling and the house seemed to have fallen into ruin. The backs of the roofs on the stables and the outhouses were all broken. It was left to Alison and I, the Bluffer's knees were not up to it by then, to climb up to the top of Jones Pumwern's hill to scatter the ashes in a glade where my mother used to go for her afternoon walk.

Alison was married from the house. The villagers lined up in a crowd to watch as she came out of the church in Pennal. After the service we had a meal at the house. But there was no dancing because the Bluffer said the English don't dance at weddings. She made her getaway in a boat across the river to the other side where there was a fast sports car waiting.

In the war time pictures the Bluffer looks thin and grave. He is aware of his considerable responsibilities. There are several pictures of him next to Ambrose McGonigal, known as Mac, who became a High Court judge in Belfast, and who will feature later in this story.

After the war the Bluffer says he was offered a place on a boat that was going to sail the Atlantic but turned it down. We were also going to emigrate to Rhodesia, which in truth would probably have suited us well.

Later in his life, when they were in Ireland, the photos show that his hair has turned silver. There is also a twinkle in the eye and he is a much more likeable man.

I study carefully the album containing Alison's wedding photos taken at Llugwy Hall. The Bluffer fits the part he is playing at the time. He is the minor industrialist, rather leaden and overweight, with views to match. He has bought a big house and is in with the local gentry. But if he doesn't watch out he is going to take a tumble.

The third time we went back to Llugwy Hall, this time without Alison, was to scatter the Bluffer's ashes.

We stood on the side of the hill in the sodden rain. There were a dozen of us, family and close friends. We looked out over the River Dyfi as it snaked its way down to the sea. It was wild and dark. Am I the only one left alive who is aware of the importance of the River Dyfi in the life of the Bluffer and my mother?

This is how it all happened.

We have been in Wales about three years. In my late teens I am back and forth. Alison has already gone to Northern Ireland. She is married and starting a family. So most of the time it is just the Bluffer and my mother.

The normal optimism and confidence which the Bluffer exudes has disappeared. A depressed air has settled over the house. This is because there have been serious mistakes and the clothing business is about to go under.

The Bluffer looks as if he is about to go under as well. He comes home for his lunch in those days. He sits in the kitchen with his cold sausages and pickles and beer.

He seems to be sinking before our eyes. He gets up at four in the morning to turn over the vegetable garden as the sun comes up. He is trying to calm his mind.

In those early morning hours, when the rest of the world was still asleep, he was also, I now realise, working on Counterpart. He was researching, asking questions, composing his stories. I asked my mother about it shortly before she died. She replied that she could always tell his mood by the rhythm of the keys as he typed.

The Bluffer never talked about this part of his life. None of us knew what he was doing. When we asked my mother she said he was writing about the old days during the war. We had no idea of the depth of his researches.

Then finally he's out of the business, one step ahead of the receivers. For a moment we can all breathe again.

Then, never proud, he is going to buy a launderette. But instead he settles for a building where he can let out some flats. On the ground floor is a bookies called Mid Wales Turf Accountants. This is run by Bronwen Evans, who is later recruited for the hotel.

'Bloody dangerous business turf accounting.' He closes his eyes as he remembers. 'If you didn't lay off properly you could go under, just like that. Crowd of bloody sharks circling round.'

But all the time he has other ideas.

Then he comes home one evening to find a stranger sitting in his chair.

When he asks my mother who this certain gentleman might be, she replies, with equal courtesy, that he had knocked at the door asking if this was the establishment that offered bed and breakfast. ( There had been a confusion with the farm run by Jones Gwerniago nearby). But my mother, being practical and knowing we needed the money, said yes of course and please do come in.

And that, the Bluffer says, is how the idea for the hotel was born.

Well not quite.

They had actually been planning it for some time.

They had surveyed the house from the lawn on summer evenings and talked quietly. They could certainly run it as a hotel but they needed money for the conversion. There were also debts from the business that needed to be paid off. So over bacon and egg suppers they did their sums. They knew it would work if they went upmarket and ran it like a country house. But for that they need to alter bedrooms, convert outhouses and upgrade kitchens. Right at the moment this is all way beyond their means.

They go to see the bank, but the bank isn't interested. Financially speaking they are in queer street.

So all that summer the Bluffer paces up and down looking for a solution.

His back is to the wall. His capital is exhausted. He can barely put food on the table. The betting shop is a liability. He is very vulnerable. Some of the smarter punters already smell blood. If a big bet comes in at the last minute and is not laid off in time the ruin will be complete.

But actually the Bluffer is good when he is in a position like this. He hunkers down, eyes dark, shoulders swaying.

I have the old war time pictures on the desk in front of me as I write. The face is serious, stern. He calls himself a Liberal Imperialist. Another era and Lawrence would have recruited him, and Mac as well, for his exploits in Arabia. A generation before that and he would have gone out to India and ruled admirably.

My mother bless her, the wisest of the wise, leaves him alone to brood and think.

Then the heaviness which he has accumulated as an industrialist starts to drop off him. He cuts down on his drinking and starts to go for long walks down by the river.

He is measuring distances and depths seeing where there could be a problem. He goes down to Aberdyfi where the river runs into the sea and measures depths there. He studies tide charts and weather maps. He goes out on a boat and explores angles of entry into the port. He never discusses what he is doing, not even with my mother, until the plan is complete.

Who was in the team? Well Bert the cockney sparra who'd done a bit of porridge. Bert drove a motorbike and he was our mechanical engineer genius.

Then there was Malcolm who worked in the packing department at the factory and who had a wife who drank. The Bluffer said she was a cretin. Today Malcolm would be classed as a sex offender. But in those days people simply knew to keep their children away from him.

There was also skinny Bronwen from the bookies who could calculate odds quicker than anyone. And Tug Roberts who'd been torpedoed on a merchant man in the war and his son Alfie. They were our handymen. The Bluffer said Tug was the salt of the earth but the last time we saw him he had a mask over his face and couldn't breathe because he'd smoked too many cigarettes.

There were other people who came and went from the house whose names I have long forgotten now. The Bluffer said at the time there were two things missing from the war. A Leica camera ( which he'd fingered himself in Germany) and his old army compass but he never said who he suspected of pinching them.

Actually they weren't his most precious asset at all. His most precious asset was a pair of pyjamas made from the silk parachute with which he'd parachuted into Yugoslavia. I found them scrunched up in a ball in a chest after he died and gave them to Jack Chambre, his great grandson, as a souvenir.

Who else was in the team? I recall Cerys Jones who became the cook at the hotel. The Bluffer said she always clanked when she was taken home at the end of the evening because of the bottles attached under her coat. Then there was our housekeeper Megan whose husband worked on the railways. The Bluffer said he always voted socialist. And then there was Glenys who lived on the other side of the river and who had to be rowed over in a boat for work in the morning.

When he came out of Yugoslavia (weight nine stone, I know all the detail) he got a lift back on a tank landing ship that was going into Bari harbour. This was when, unknowingly, he passed Tug Roberts, at the time on a merchant ship, who was coming out of Bari harbour.

The way the Bluffer recounts it there was a hell of a whammpphh and the walls of the wardroom where he was taking a tincture with the bosun bent in and out.

This was the explosion on the Liberty Ship in Bari harbour in April 1945. Hundreds of people were killed. According to the Bluffer they stacked up the naked bodies, which had all turned blue, on the dockside.

But here is where the Bluffer says he made his mistake. When he was parachuted into Yugoslavia he was given a special belt which contained a quantity of gold sovereigns. These were for bribing the locals and he didn't use them all. 'I should have kept them,' the Bluffer told me. 'An opportunity like that only comes up once in a life time.'

So when he looked out over the river he would have said to himself, ' I'm not going to waste another opportunity like that. A river's a useful thing. Do alright with that.'

The final straw with the business had been the Spanish enterprise. The Bluffer had taken the wrong advice and gone half shares in a clothing company in Barcelona. 'Seduced by the lure of cheap cloth,' he says sadly and shakes his head. 'Bloody awful workmanship. Stuff stitched back to front, arse ways round, upside down and all sorts.' The Bluffer shakes his head again. But with the Bluffer nothing is ever wasted.

He spends his days off in Barcelona noseying around. The Bluffer makes contacts wherever he goes. People talk to him, he finds things out. So he discovers that the Spanish fisherman's lot is not a happy one. Then he's on an errand in the back streets and happens on a warehouse with good Spanish brandy for sale at discount prices. He stores all the information away.

When he has finished surveying the river he takes Bert up and down the coast looking at boats. In the end, south of Aberystwyth, they find a twenty four footer that the Bluffer thinks will do the job. They take her out for a trial. She's open and a few years old but the draft is shallow enough so she'll be manoeuvrable on the river. They'll just have to be careful on the open sea. Bert puts the engine through its paces. Then he strips it down and says it's in good condition.

But the Bluffer hesitates. He wonders if it will be sturdy enough. Finally he rings Pat Twining who used to work at the factory and knows about boats. He comes down and taps the timbers and then looks at the shape of the hull and says they will be safe enough in that. After that they motor slowly up the coast and moor up in Aberdyfi. Then the Bluffer flies to Spain and spends a week spying out his old contacts. When he returns he is in excellent humour and tells my mother, ' I think we may just have solved our little problems.'

## 6

A death is always a good time for looking back.

Yesterday I went into the kitchen of our house in Cornwall and studied the pestle and mortar that Supin used every day to grind up her spices. It came in the suitcase with her from Thailand.

Then I went into the living room where on the wall above the fireplace there are two good sized portraits of the King and Queen of Thailand. They are still in their youthful vigour.

I am certainly not a monarchist, rather the other way in fact, but those pictures have been with us for thirty years and they were important to Supin, so they stay up.

The puzzle is that while I am older by those thirty odd years, the figures in the pictures have not changed at all. Their Royal presences have not altered. For them time means something different.

Supin's earliest memory is riding on her mother's back. They are walking along a path in the country. Her mother is making her laugh by telling her a story about a tiger who lives in the jungle.

There is a lot of family history here. Supin's father died when she was four. He was a gambler too and after the death her mother went to work in a saw mill. That was in the country near Nakhon Nayok. But whatever money came in it wasn't sufficient to raise five children.

But here, though she may not have realised it at the time, Supin had a stroke of luck. She was sent to live with a family in Bangkok and she went, as far as I can work it out, from living a poor life in the country to joining the elite. Really she shot up from bottom to top.

Mr Thamnong and his wife and their four children had a lovely big house in the Sukhumvit area of the city. I went back there once and met Mrs Thamnong but by then she was very frail. When Mr Thamnong died Supin flew home to attend the funeral. That was several years before Parkinson's disease was diagnosed.

But there is no doubt about it. We have checked his memoir against the internet. He may not have been as important as the Prime Minister or the Foreign Minister or the Defense Minister but in the 1970s Thamnong Singalavanich was Deputy Minister of Agriculture and Co-operatives. So Supin went from being a poor country girl to growing up in the house of a government minister. All this is true.

We have an official portrait photograph of him on the wall and I get up to look at it now.

Mr Thamnong is certainly a man aware of his importance. Anyone can see that. He has all the braid, all the medals, all the scrambled egg.

But he also has the air of a sensitive and intelligent man who would have tried to educate his people. I am sure he would have been a good father or step father, or guardian.

Supin always laughs when she talks about him.

She says he drove a wooden panelled Morris Minor shooting brake and that when he arrived home from trips abroad he always gave her the small jars of mustard and marmalade that he had been served on the plane.

Because of Mr Thamnong, she says, she dreamt of flying in a plane and visiting foreign countries and because of me all these dreams came true.

There is also a second photograph, this one in black and white, which shows Mr Thamnong kneeling, head bowed, as the king awards him a decoration.

This morning I opened up Mr Thamnong's memoir. That is the first time I have ever done that. The pages crackle as I turn them. Supin must have been looking at it shortly before she died because there are still flowers in it that have not lost all their colour.

Then I can see she has been guiding me. She knew I would come to the memoir eventually. There is a Bird of Paradise plant that still sits in the corner of our living room. She has used the flowers to mark certain pages with photographs. I turn a page and stop.

So there you are! I certainly recognise that cheeky little face at the back of the family group. How old were you then? Ten, twelve? Well there it is. That is a pleasure. I shall treasure that. The earliest picture. I am sure people who know they are going to die often set up little surprises for those they leave behind.

***

When we lived in Bangkok, right at the beginning, we had two rooms in a wooden house and cooked over a charcoal fire outside. If he had seen it the Bluffer would certainly have given a little frown and said, ' Well perhaps not the best part of town.'

One day after I had got paid, in a flush of prosperity, I went to the shop at the end of the soi and bought a two ring electric burner for us to cook on. I was just trying to advance us into the 20th century.

Then one evening I was writing a letter home to the Bluffer and my mother describing life in this strange country. Supin was watching over my shoulder. When I finished the letter she picked it up and studied it and then said, with a laugh, "My God, I think a chicken just run over your paper."

There were times before the illness got too difficult that she went back to visit by herself. But people said she had changed because she lived in England. They told her she had become European. By that they meant she was more direct and pushy. She used to laugh about that when she came home.

All the pictures from that time are in front of me now.

There is one of Duk our scrappy mongrel dog. His real name was the Duke of Wellington, but only he and I knew that. I took him for a walk up the soi every evening on his lead. This amused our neighbours.

On occasion the boys who played football in front of the house invited me to join them. There is a picture of that as well.

Then one evening they squared off the compound for a cock fight. There are pictures of the boys holding the cockerels. I am surprised at how young they are. Everyone seems to be laughing.

These are all good memories.

But an unpleasant surprise awaits when I open another packet of pictures in the same file.

There are a dozen black and white shots and they show the bodies of two young men who have been executed in a prison yard.

A neighbour in our little compound who worked in the prison, who knew that I was a journalist, took them himself and I bought them from him.

When we moved to Ireland I sold them in turn to an agency and I have seen them in several magazines since. I study the pictures closely.

The poor men, they were caught smuggling drugs across the border from Cambodia, have been strung up on some awful contraption and then machine gunned in the back. I find it shocking now to think that I sold those pictures.

The next packet of photos shows us on the beach at Hua Hin. We are in front of a wooden cabin with the sea in the background. I have got a bottle of beer in one hand and Supin is smoking a cigarette and we are both laughing but I have no recollection of what the joke was.

## 7

This is how the Bluffer deploys his troops.

Bronwen from Mid Wales Turf Accountants is placed in the car on the front at Aberdyfi. Her job is to flash out the agreed signals, via the car headlights, to the Spanish trawler waiting in the bay. The Bluffer is in the boat with Bert. Tug Roberts, our handyman, is also on board. The boat, repainted black so nothing shows, is riding low in the water. The Bluffer and his crew are blacked up as well. It is dead o' night. Slight swell, no moon. They are now two miles from the rendezvous.

Then the Bluffer picks out the lights of the Spanish trawler and turns and calls out quietly to his men that they are about to come alongside.

In a minute Tug Roberts grabs a rope and then the Bluffer is up a ladder and being greeted by the Spanish skipper. Then the cases of brandy are handed down. This is a first run, a test run, so there is not a full load. After a quarter of an hour they push off again. As they approach the shore the Bluffer stares ahead searching for the signal from Bronwen. When it comes he breathes a sigh of relief and tells Bert to take her in.

It's always a dead o' night job with the Bluffer.

Half way up the river Bert cuts the engine and the Bluffer take one oar and Tug Roberts takes the other. The Bluffer calls out the rhythm in a whisper, one two, one two. That is the way they make their way slowly up river. Rowlocks are muffled and they are praying that the moon will not come out to expose them.

Malcolm is standing on the lawn to take the painter and tie her up. Then all the rest of the gang come down and we all set to and unload her. After that we ship the booty into an outhouse and the following morning the Bluffer sets off to Birmingham to sell it on, coming home with a thick roll of bank notes in his back pocket and a satisfied grin on his face.

The set up works perfectly. But the Bluffer is wise. Never mess up a good thing, he says. Don't do it too often.

Then one night there is a crisis.

The moon is slipping in and out between the clouds and there is a heavy swell in the bay. The transfer has not been easy. One of the Spanish fishermen catches his wrist as the boats plunge up and down and suddenly the skipper is shouting angrily from the bridge. If the sea had been any higher they would have had to abandon the transfer. But eventually they push off from the trawler and turn for home.

The Bluffer is already standing up and peering ahead through his night glasses to spot the outline of the port and Bronwen's signal when Tug Roberts taps him on the shoulder and points to his left and the Bluffer turns round to see the darkened shape of a boat approaching.

It's about half a mile off and closing fast. He can make out a sharp bow wave.

Then a bright searchlight is switched on and the beam is sweeping the sea in front of them. The Bluffer signals to Bert to cut the engine and they crouch down and wait. The search light flips over them once but misses them. The next time it is nearer. It is then that the Bluffer takes a decision.

His old service pistol has lain unused in a drawer for twenty years. But before beginning this operation he has taken it out and oiled it and got a small amount of ammunition discreetly from an old army contact and spent an hour in the woods behind the house practising until his old skills returned.

The pursuing boat is closing. The Bluffer stands up quickly and braces himself, legs apart, against the swell. He waits for the range to close and then takes steady aim and fires at the engine block. Immediately the noise of the engine changes and the searchlight dances into the sky as if in surprise and he fires quickly again, this time taking out the searchlight and plunging the scene into comforting darkness. Then he ducks down and signals to Bert to open her up and they head to the coast at top speed.

Fortune generally favours the brave and that night it certainly favoured the Bluffer and his men. Because they had a full load on they were low in the water. At the same time they were showing no lights, the moon was covered, the night was dark and they were well blacked up. So they would have been a difficult target to spot. There was also enough of a swell to deter anyone else from being out on the water.

On a normal night they would have used the engine to bring them up the river to the first houses. But that night the Bluffer would not allow it. Instead they rowed hard all the way. The Bluffer called out the stroke and they changed places every ten minutes. The banks of the river slid by them. They could hear the odd car go past and saw a late night train. Lights were still on in several houses. The Bluffer fingered his gun and hoped to God he would not have to use it again. As they came around the last bend and the house came into sight they stopped and the Bluffer scoped the lawn with his night glasses. There was a light on in my mother's bedroom. He checked the rest of the lawn. Quickly he picked out the shape of Malcolm waiting by the boat house. But to his relief he could not see any welcoming party of Customs officers.

They tied up and the rest of the gang appeared as usual and they started to unload the boxes. Normally they would have been stored in one of the outhouses and the Bluffer would have taken them on the following day. But he knew he had to move quickly that night. So he went into the house and explained to my mother what had happened and she, God bless her, came out in her dressing gown and helped us, we were working by torchlight, to get the truck loaded up. After that the Bluffer hid the gun and then climbed up into the cab and set off, going by side lights on minor roads until he was well clear of the area.

When he returned the following evening, over several large whiskeys, he recounted to my mother what had happened and they made a decision to suspend operations for a time. They also made the assumption that it had been a Customs boat although they were never questioned or investigated.

As they waited my mother and the Bluffer did their calculations. They were surprised at how well they had done in such a short space of time. The Bluffer said wistfully that at the rate they were going they wouldn't need to open a hotel at all.

This was one of the few occasions when The Bluffer had the Riot Act read to him by my mother. She told him that it had been a narrow escape and there must be a time limit on future operations.

# 8

The progression of Parkinson's disease is not inevitable.

On occasion when we saw John Gibson at Derriford Hospital I asked him where we were going but he always said, quite rightly, that every case was different and that a forecast was impossible.

In Supin's case the initial symptoms are a certain stiffness and clumsiness.

There are also occasions when she freezes completely. If this happens she has to stop and wait for the medication to free her up.

The principle drug she takes is Sinemet. This is the drug which has released the inhibitions and drawn her into the world of the casino.

A further side effect of the Sinemet is that it causes a series of involuntary movements known as dyskinesia. As the years pass and the dosage of the Sinemet is increased so this involuntary movement, a sort of twitching and jerking, will become almost continuous.

The disease, and the medication, are also causing other changes. Supin's moods can now swing suddenly, leading at times to very erratic behaviour. But she is still beautiful and she can still light up a room with a smile.

We closed the restaurant two years ago and we now spend a lot of our time in the casino on Union Street.

The gaming room is equipped with both Roulette and Blackjack tables. The lighting is low and the decor indeterminate. The exception is the small bar and restaurant area which is fitted out in dark wood covered over with a bright pink flock.

The staff - all the croupiers, pit bosses, managers, bar men, waitresses - wear white shirts, gold coloured waistcoats and black bow ties.

The characters who populate these casinos are a rich seam for a writer to mine.

The two who had the most influence on us were Ivor Dryer, who ended up figuring in all the national newspapers, and George Lynes who became our intelligence officer. There was also Jackie, the Chinese head waiter, and Mr Chong.

Supin's confidence is steadily being chipped away by the Parkinson's disease. But when she is on a winning streak at the casino she can regain, for a moment, some of the lightness that she had before.

I am watching her at the table now. I note with pleasure the gesture with the fingers. There is the half turn of the head, the innocent smile, which is almost a laugh. I approach and she palms me a handful of chips which I take over to the desk and cash in.

But I am always careful not to interrupt a winning streak. If I do say something, however innocuous, and on the next spin she loses, I will be blamed for breaking the run. These interruptions can be imagined as well as real.

But by now I can judge what she needs. When she is hungry I order coffee and sandwiches. She generally eats at the table when she is playing. When she needs to take a tablet I tell the waitress to bring a glass of water.

I would not suggest it to John Gibson as any sort of remedy but there is no doubt that the twitching and shaking which are beginning to plague her by then do stop when she is concentrating at the Roulette or Blackjack table.

It is always a pleasure going home when Supin wins.

She takes money out of her purse and I stop the car and buy fish and chips. But she can never wait until we get home, she has to eat straightaway in the car as we drive. I look over and see a little smile playing on her face as she eats. When we finally arrive at the house she counts out how much money she has won.

We are sitting at the kitchen table but the explanation for her success has become so complicated she has confused even herself. We stare at the money piled up in front of us. Is this really some minor miracle?

These are the times when I turn to my sad, wonderful, magical wife, and wonder if she is not, after all, an eccentric mathematical genius.

I have described what Supin was like when she won but what was she like when she lost, when she had gone down every avenue and had blown the lot and was completely cleaned out?

Well then she is a completely different person.

All the nerves that should be on the inside of her skin are suddenly transposed to the outside.

She cooks strange foods, worries about her teeth, smokes cigarettes without inhaling, walks about the house at four in the morning, puts her arm in a sling and moves her bed next to the radiator in the living room. She has migraine headaches and becomes constipated. She develops illnesses that doctors have never heard of. The blame for her predicament is placed on others. She stops talking. She moves the furniture around, she demands a divorce, she looks out of the window from a kneeling position, wears startlingly odd combinations of clothes and refuses to take off her hat.

Then finally, when she is ready, the whole fine mess into which she has got herself is admitted. Coughs are given and instructions issued not to be angry. Then from the bottom of one of the dozen handbags she uses, bills and bank statements are drawn out. There are odd scraps of paper on which calculations have been made, there are notes from pawnshops, IOUs, bank passbooks opened and closed, receipts from ATM machines, letters from debt collecting agencies. It is all spread out on the table and working together we sort it out. A settlement is reached.

When that has been done a period of calm descends on our house.

Meals are substantial and sleep patterns regularise themselves. There is probably a visit to the Thai temple at Kings Bromley in Staffordshire. She likes to spend time with the Abbot, Phra Maha Laow, who we know well.

She has every intention of keeping to the repayment terms imposed. But after a few weeks the detail of what has been agreed becomes blurred on both sides. There are other occasions though when she repays the money the following week. She comes home from the casino her purse proudly bulging with notes. On those occasions, with everything back to normal, we dine out and are both happy once again.

We make friends with all sorts and types at the casino. The roulette wheel does not recognise social or cultural divides. We are soon on first name terms with a leading city architect, a cardiac surgeon at Derriford Hospital and a retired psychiatrist and his Iranian wife.

A picture of the city architect comes into my mind as I write this now.

When he first came into the casino he always wore a suit and he carried himself with a certain authority. But the last time I saw him the suit had been replaced by an ill fitting sweater and he was thinner and quite broken and bent over. But he still continued his daily duty of pushing his chips out on to the green baize of the roulette table.

Though they never met the Bluffer would certainly have got on well with George Lynes.

They would have recognised each other immediately. Raffles meets Liverpool Scally. Both secretly despising the law abiding middle classes.

George was from Liverpool and I suppose in his sixties by then. He was small and stout and walked awkwardly due to a badly treated hernia. Even though he always dressed in a dark suit and white shirt with open collar he still had the overall form of a rather shapeless bloodhound. But he had spent twenty years working as a croupier and a pit boss so he knew the casino business as well as anyone.

It was George who warned Supin about getting involved with Ivor Dryer.

Jackie, who had collar length hair and a face that was so open as to be slightly absent looking, was head waiter at a Chinese restaurant on New George Street. One evening when the casino was offering a free buffet he laid a table specially for us, with white cloth and all the correct cutlery and served us as if we were in his restaurant. Neither Supin nor I had any idea why he did it.

There were people who avoided Jackie, saying he was not all there and brought them bad luck, but that was simply the guise under which he operated. Really he observed and noted everything.

Old Mr Chong was white haired, mild mannered and spoke very broken English. Jackie said he had spent many years in jail in Hong Kong. He became the armourer to our group for the adventures that followed.

Certainly our consultant neurologist John Gibson would have been astonished to find himself bracketed in such company, but he was the one handing out the tablets. He was the one making it all happen.

## 9

The Bluffer was a generous man. There was not a mean bone in his body. If he had a fault it was that he could not contain his enthusiasms. He was like an incoming tide, he swept all before him.

The only time he became annoyed was when his advice, having being sought, was not taken. If this happened he would bristle. This was a strange sort of pose. His head would go back and a look of startled surprise would cross his face.

The Bluffer could also bristle if he was upstaged during conversation. He would give way to someone of a superior social category to himself, such as a judge or a bishop, but anyone else he would fight for supremacy.

The Bluffer was also a very tall man, standing, as he was always proud to point out, at six foot four and a half inches. My mother by contrast was tiny, barely over five feet.

I have two pictures of them on the desk in front of me now.

My mother is standing on a bench so as to be level with him. The pictures are taken fifty years apart, but the expressions are still the same - the same grin, the same joke, about the difference in height, still being shared.

I am in Northern Ireland now. The Bluffer has been dead several weeks and I am starting to work my way through his papers. The filing cabinet to my left, so chock full of his words, has now moved another degree or so off the vertical. If I leave it any longer the draws will jam and I will need a crow bar to force them open.

The face the Bluffer offers to the world and the face revealed here are startlingly different.

As I start to go through the files I see that he has been casting about restlessly.

I enter the labyrinth at a point where he seems worried and anxious, the slightest trifle bothering him and setting him off on a new path.

I discover a copy of the Shropshire Lad underlined and dog eared and with his notes added in pencil in the margin. I stop and look out of the window again. I remember him reading it to me as a boy.

He always liked the country. He was happy there. He hated towns. Whenever we moved to a new house he would select a patch for his vegetable garden. But he was never sentimental about it. He never talked about the earth running through his fingers or anything like that. But he was always proud when he could announce that all the vegetables on our plates at dinner had come from his garden. Supin was the same. Before she got ill she would spend all day in the garden.

There are dozens of files and hundreds of notes and letters. There are old diaries which I flick through. Here he has written of Alison after she has gone into hospital for more treatment, ‘ She is a woman of great courage who I love and admire.’

He was heartbroken when she died before him. But I was the only one who saw his tears.

I flick through for entries at the time Supin and I got married. Here he is a week after the wedding. ‘ An interesting and unique addition to the family. The future will certainly be interesting!’

Then I open an envelope and find his thoughts on Handel’s Messiah. But he has been thinking and writing quickly and it is difficult to read. The only phrase I can make out is his regret at never having learned to play a musical instrument.

His hand writing is curiously unformed. There is not the rolling elegance one might except of someone so easily at home with words, written or oral. It is really still the hand of a boy.

As I dip further down I have the feeling that this verbiage is just a cover.

There is a file of correspondence with engineers over wind pumps and solar panels. At this point he typed most of his letters and he has kept the carbons.

At a later date he has become interested in something called the Stirling Engine and there are a series of e mails which he has printed out. He is in contact with an engineer in Sweden and is suggesting certain changes that he thinks will be an improvement.

He loves engines, pumps, all things mechanical that go in and out and up and down. He told me that when he was a boy he wanted to be a ship’s captain or an auctioneer. Perhaps he should have been an inventor. But really he should have been a policeman. He is always on watch, never missing a trick.

The Bluffer loves to correspond with important people. Here he has written to the Archbishop of Canterbury. He says he has been to a funeral service at St Mary Redcliffe in Bristol and he wants to commend the address of the vicar which he thought was first class. The Archbishop replies in his own hand to say he knows the vicar in question well and is not surprised that he gave a good address. A short correspondence between the two men then follows.

But the Bluffer isn't really a churchman. He always went to the Armistice Day service but it was only in the last years of his life that he wore his medals.

There are several copies of letters he has written to the Times. There are also articles which he has sent in which have been returned as unsuitable for publication.

I open up one file and see he has begun a novel. I am surprised at how good it is.

There is a long section where he is captain of a tramp steamer. He has to keep watch on the bridge all night as they round Cape Horn. The detail is extensive. He must have spent hours with maps and charts. The voyage starts in Liverpool in what he calls ' dirty weather. ' Half way across the Atlantic they spot icebergs to the North and the sea starts to get up but they make it in to New York without mishap. After that they go down the Eastern Seaboard of the United States stopping over in the Falklands to discharge timber. Then they round Cape Horn and head toward Australia.

There are pages of great tenderness which I think are really a love letter to my mother.

In another file he has described how he was in Germany after the war interviewing Russian prisoners desperate to come over.

I pick up a copy of the Daily Telegraph obituary which is beside me. Amidst all the other stuff this is dealt with in one sentence:

'He was then posted to Minden in western Germany, where he interrogated deserters from the Soviet forces who were suspected of being agents posing as refugees.'

There is a file where this is described in considerable detail. He has noted the haggard looks on the faces of the prisoners, the desperate pleas not to be returned home. At the conclusion of this section he has typed, 'I don't care if half of them were spies. It is with great pride I report that I did not return a single one of those men.'

There are letters to me, written but never posted, expressing puzzlement and disappointment. These I take out into the garden and burn. All fathers are disappointed by their sons so that is nothing new. There are lists of old girlfriends with all sorts of detail which I decline to read.

To begin with he has tried to keep the files in order but as I dig down I can see they are becoming more jumbled. On the front of one file, in exasperation, he has written, 'This is just a bloody mess!'

After a couple of hours I need a break from all these files and the thousands of words they contain.

I go outside and see that in the raised beds the small harvest is coming through. I pick lettuce and spring onions for lunch and eat a sandwich at the desk, one eye on the sloping filing cabinet to my side.

After the death of my mother he started to look up old girl friends. There is a correspondence with an elderly lady living in Wales but it doesn't look as if anything has come from it.

I keep digging through the papers, occasionally diverting to his bookshelves or to other files on his computer or to other internet sites. The Bluffer's mind at this point has been darting everywhere. Is he looking for something or trying to recall an event? He is getting frustrated. Stuffed down the side of the armchair where he sits I find a copy of Dr Zhivago along with a bottle opener and a postcard, unwritten and unstamped, showing the new airport in Hong Kong.

There are pages and pages of accounts and figures crossed out and recalculated. He seems to be concerned about a rise in the price of gas. The size of his phone bill is bothering him too. He has written on the front of the statement, 'Must be more careful in future.' Why does the Bluffer always worry so much about money? His bonds and shares, which I will inherit, show he is in good financial order. The Bluffer has been prudent over the years and has left a decent sum.

The reason he worries is because he never really got over the failure of the clothing business in Wales. He was always conscious of money after that. The bust had hurt him deeply. It was also his generation. The war generation. Mend and make do whether you are rich or poor. When you have been through that you are always careful with money. And quite right too. People of my generation are far too profligate.

Because the Bluffer is careful with his money I am surprised, going through his accounts, to find that he has run up some credit card debts. Not a lot but still it is unlike him. I can pay them off easily enough. I work my way down the statement interested to see what he has been spending his money on. I stop when I see that he has booked a flight to Munich but then apparently cancelled it at the last minute. Attached to the statement is a printed out e mail correspondence where he has been trying to get his money back from the airline. No dice there Bluffer.

There are pages of recipes, book preferences, he has even been scouting around the internet for the best way to darn a sock.

Then he is considering backing a new project to drill wells in Africa. I check back. It's the same engineer he has been in correspondence with in Sweden over the redesign of the Stirling Engine. He has noted in the margin of one of the letters, 'At last something sensible.'

Digging further down I find he has been writing to the Minister of Education suggesting changes to the school curriculum. But when I read what he is proposing I am disappointed to see how unoriginal it is, essentially a return to the eleven plus and learning by rote. For a moment I am reminded of the period when he ran the factory. He was the minor industrialist, carrying too much weight, convinced that his rather leaden views were somehow diamonds or pearls of wisdom that had never been exposed to the light of day before.

Sometimes, he writes, he goes into the garden at night and listens to the wind in the trees and knows that he can hear my mother speaking. He says they have conversations and she describes what it is like in heaven.

There are times when he records that he feels very lonely and cut off. It has got worse since his eyes deteriorated and the doctor stopped him from driving. He says the worst moment is the late afternoon when the light is starting to go and before there is anything decent on the television.

There is a cachet of love letters my mother wrote to him before they were married which I still cannot bear to open.

There are also several files of newspaper clippings which I go through briefly but for the moment I cannot find the thread of what connects the articles together.

The Bluffer records almost no details about his health though he suffers with several painful conditions. He has had an ulcer on his leg for six months which won't heal. A nurse comes to dress it twice a week. But his comments are on the nurse rather than his leg. If she could see what he has written, she would certainly blush. But then he says that he is old and that he is going to do die soon and so the state of his health does not worry him at all.

He is darting backward and forward. He has made a brief study of the lives of the charcoal burners of the Forest of Dean. He is interested in the way they live. My only two points of reference for the Forest of Dean are the playwright Dennis Potter and the writer Laurie Lee, but I don't recall ever discussing them with the Bluffer.

I am surprised how quickly he can change tack.

There is a slim file of newspaper clippings which show he is becoming exercised about the number of Nigerian women arriving in Dublin to give birth to their babies so they can claim Irish citizenship.

He has scrawled in the margin of one of the articles, 'Has anyone calculated the cost of this? No wonder the bloody country is broke.'

His restless mind is going back and forward. His bluff exterior is only a cover. Underneath he is always anxious.

Here, for some reason, he has become critical of the BBC.

There is a carbon of a letter he has sent to the Director General which he has concluded by saying, ' It is quite obvious to me that the Brown Hatters and the Nancy Boys are still in charge at the BBC!'

Sometimes I have to take a break from all this.

One afternoon with rain barring my normal afternoon walk I turned on the television to watch Peter Snow and his son Dan discussing their lives.

It seems that everything I do these days gives me a clue to the Bluffer - and on occasion to Supin and sometimes to Alison and to my mother.

Peter and Dan Snow are similar to the Bluffer. They are full of enthusiasms. I watch the easy way they toss things around. They have sailed the Atlantic, written books, made their television programmes, done dozens of other things.

The Bluffer said that the headmaster of his school wanted to educate his boys to be Liberal Imperialists.

I can't take my eyes off the Snows, pere and fils. They are as much Liberal Imperialists as the Bluffer. I am certain of that.

And of course under that easy façade they are swimming like mad. The Snow household must have been a very odd sort of place. I turn off the television and go back into the office.

There are pages and pages of material.

For some reason he has been casting around the internet to see if he can buy a motorbike with a side car.

Then there is a folder which contains pictures of a woman and a man on what seems to be a cruise ship.

I examine the faces closely. The man means nothing to me but the shape of the woman's face is familiar. There is something there from a long time ago, a faint outline. I examine the background of the pictures to see if there is any indication of where the ship is moored.

In several of the photos both the husband and wife are wearing coats. I hold the photos up to the light. They are photocopies on to A4 paper.

There are pictures of them dining, then they are walking on the deck looking over the side. What are they up to?

I had assumed that it was the woman who had sent the photos, but it could have been the man. I presume they have been sent to the Bluffer. I look at the envelope but it is not the one the photos were sent in. Perhaps he wanted to disguise the handwriting or the postmark.

The pictures are marked one, two, three, four, so there is obviously a sequence but I can't find the key anywhere.

My sister Alison has a recollection. She always laughs when she tells the story. She is eight so I am four. Our mother is throwing cushions at the Bluffer and using words she doesn't understand. Then I have a memory too. One afternoon when my mother was elderly and needed a stick to steady herself we went for a walk down the avenue at Ballyarr, the house where they were living then in the Irish Republic.

We stopped to turn and look back up to the house. We were talking about the Bluffer. We always talked about him. My mother adored him. I am sure he was an easy man for women to adore. Then she said ' I don't care if he has looked at other women...' but then she changed the subject and the sentence was never finished.

Was it with this memory to hand that she went back and painted those furiously vivid pictures that hang in my front room at home in Cornwall?

The Bluffer's mind can change direction very quickly. Here he has been following the news.

There has been an incident in the Middle East and in a note attached to a clipping he has recorded something rather unkind, the usual sort of stuff, against the Jews. Then he has switched his attention to the Muslims.

But here he has shown his ingenuity. In a pamphlet, complete with illustrations, he has described a different way to butcher cattle that he says should meet Halal religious and cultural requirements but that will also be kinder to the animal.

And so it goes on.

He keeps a table of all movements of wildlife in the garden and records dates when trees blossom and flowers start to bud. Every morning he taps the barometer and notes the pressure. He says by studying this information he can provide meteorlogical forecasts as accurate as anything on the BBC.

But all the time I know he is going deeper and deeper swimming past obstacles and reefs. He is sinking down, the water is now filthy and muddy. Soon if he keeps going he will be resting on the bottom.

Finally I pull open the lowest drawer of the filing cabinet. I look down to see a thick manila envelope. Below that there is a faded red folder. In this folder, I know, at last, that I will find the manuscript of Counterpart. This is the book he spent years writing. I put the manila envelope on the desk first. Then leaning down I get both hands around the faded red folder and lift it up. Even now it is heavy and when I put it down onto the table I can feel the legs settling.

# 10

Gamblers are poets and dreamers. They have moments of extraordinary clarity and intuition. But there are other moments of terrible miscalculation and disaster.

When I am feeling optimistic I call them the Rainbow Chasers. But on other occasions I am more critical. This is when it is obvious to me that their schemes and hunches are actually so much fantasy and humbug. Then I see them all for what they are.

After that I stay away, perhaps for weeks on end, and have a bit of a breather and leave them to it.

But every gambler has a moment to remember.

For Supin it was one winter's night when she made her attempt to hunt down that elusive rainbow and claim her own pot of gold.

On occasion we still drove past the old restaurant and it saddened us to see it empty and cold and shut up. It was as if it had died. But then one evening we saw that it had opened up again. Bright lights were sparkling out once more. I have often wondered whether that was the signal for which she was waiting. It is a fish restaurant and the new owners are supposed to be doing well, but we have never had the courage to step inside. We would be confronted by too many ghosts.

We had also spent a weekend at the Thai Buddhavihara temple at Kings Bromley in Staffordshire. It is a place Supin likes to go when the Parkinson's disease is starting to overwhelm her. The monks are a calming influence and she always comes away refreshed. But Supin, like all Thai people, is superstitious, so it is possible that she has picked up some sort of clue from our stay there.

She spends the afternoon getting ready.

When she finally emerges from the bedroom she is wearing a low cut silk blouse and a long tight fitting red skirt. Around her neck there is a string of pearls ( now where did she get those from?) and perched on the side of her head is a slinky little pill box hat and out of which pops, astonishingly, a bright blue peacock feather.

She walks down the stairs toward me with all the brilliance and dazzle and elegance of a mad foreign film star. There is a little smile on her lips. At that point I am sure I loved her more dearly than ever.

When we looked back later I asked her what made her so confident that night, whether she had seen the re opening of the restaurant as an omen or whether she had noted something at the temple.

But she could never give me an answer.

I concluded in the end was that it was simply an act of faith. She wanted a big win so much that she thought, somehow, she could just conjure it up.

When we entered the casino George, who had arrived ahead of us, came up to give us his scouting report.

A certain Greek croupier, who was never favourable to us, was not working that night. Two of the other Roulette tables were being operated by dealers who brought Supin luck. A Chinese man, a friend of Jackie's, had won earlier on a table by the door and a Scotsman playing Blackjack on the table nearest the restaurant claimed to have been short changed by a dealer. Aside from that it was all quiet.

Normally Supin would let three or four spins pass before she sat down to play. She needed to get the rhythm of the table. When she finally did begin she was like a miner searching for a seam of gold. She went forward carefully searching inch by inch for the elusive riches.

She could also calculate the odds quicker than I could. Later when the illness had progressed and we had given up the casino and I took her into the bingo in her wheelchair she could still play two cards at a time and keep up.

But tonight this precious routine was abandoned.

She did a quick tour of the floor, but more to show off her outfit than anything else. Then she picked a Roulette table at random, changed her money into chips and began to play.

She was nowhere near on the first two spins and I took a step back and walked around to the other side of the room.

She had got a much larger advance from me than I would normally have given and she had been elsewhere looking for additional funds.

So sufficient capital was in place to allow her to make her attempt.

But this was not a carefully judged risk. Tonight she was betting the farm. So this was either courage, skill, faith or, more likely, a form of madness.

Nothing goes unremarked in the casino. Jackie and Mr Chong, who are standing next to me, have noted that she has changed her style of play. They are watching interestedly. Faithful old George is alongside her and he looks nervous.

She leans over the table and pushes out a pile of chips on to a single number for the third play.

I have estimated that she can keep going at this level for another three or four spins. If she has not found her way in by then she will have run out of capital and she will be in serious financial trouble.

I am at the far side of the room, and though there is the normal background noise of a casino to contend with, I can still hear the ball as it spins around the wheel. Every gambler knows that moment of suspense before the ball finally drops down into a slot. As I watch my stomach turns into a tight knot. Then I see her straighten up from the table.

She catches my eye. She delays a fraction of a second. She knows exactly where I have been standing. For a terrible moment I am certain she has lost again. But then she gives that little smile and the nod of the head and I know that my mad wonderful wife has found her rhythm and that we are into the gold seam.

I unclasp my hands. Mr Chong returns to talk to Jackie. My services as banker of last resort, which undoubtedly would have been called on, will not be needed after all that night.

After that she gave a master class in working a Roulette table. I picked up the pattern of her play. She has the confidence to go for whole numbers. I know the series of numbers she uses. There is also the occasional advance up the table to zero. If there is a loss she returns to corners and splits, or even retreats to the edge of the table, until she feels ready to come back in. At one point she loses three spins in a row and takes a break to regroup. I order coffee and sandwiches to be brought to her. Her spirits revived she goes back and picks up the rhythm immediately.

For a two hour period Supin mined her seam of gold faultlessly. Other gamblers began to follow her. Soon my dear wife, in her little pill box hat with its peacock feather sticking out of the side, was the centre of attention for the whole casino.

All the time George was backwards and forwards scouting and reporting back on the action at the other tables. He whispered all the detail into her ear. I was the transporter, ferrying the winnings to the cash desk and getting twenty pound and sometimes fifty pound notes in return so that in the end my pockets were bulging.

Even a change of dealer did not put her off. But most importantly she picked the right moment to stop.

She had a win on zero and then lost twice in a row on a corner. Then she looked at George and shook her head and said,' I'm tired now, I want to go home.'

We took most of the money in the form of a cheque but at the same time our pockets were still full of cash. When we got home and counted it all up we realised that Supin had won a little over ten thousand pounds.

Supin was left completely exhausted by her efforts and spent the next two days in bed recovering. People with Parkinson's disease are capable of making great efforts, but they pay a price afterwards. Her face was grey and she slept most of the time. I was left to provide meals, check tablets and wait for her to re emerge.

Most gamblers will admit that a big win can be as destabilising as a big loss. When I look back now we were actually happiest when Supin won enough for us to have a good lunch in town the following day and with enough left over to act as seed corn for the evening.

But on this occasion, when she had recovered, she sent me down to Thomas Cook on Old Town Street to book a holiday.

I discussed various itineraries with the travel agent. We looked briefly at New York and an argument was put forward for Hawaii but in the end I returned home with tickets for Thailand, as I knew I would.

It's only a small point, but I cannot remember how we travelled up to London to get the flight.

It could be that we drove up in the old Mondeo. But it is more likely, if we had all that money, that we would have gone up with Brymon Airways. They were still doing the London run in those days.

The flight back to Thailand is clear in my memory. It was EVA Air. Everyone went home on EVA Air in those days.

Supin was laughing and joking with the stewardesses. She was in great form. With such an extraordinary win we thought that some sort of miracle had happened and she was going to recover.

The reality of our return was something of a disappointment.

When I look back now I see that we had too much money. We didn't know how to live like that. It threw us off balance.

Normally we would have stayed with friends or certainly in a hotel that was very modest.

But this time we felt obliged, with the amount of money we had won, to choose a luxurious hotel in the centre of Bangkok. But after a while we were both uncomfortable with that level of grandeur and obsequiousness.

After several days of luxury meals and some idle shopping trips we felt lost and unhappy.

So one afternoon Supin ordered a taxi from the hotel and we drove down to Khlong Toei. This at the time was a real slum area down by the docks.

Supin was talking to the taxi driver and explaining what she planned to do. I was in the back seat. I could see that the driver looked quite unhappy about it.

Eventually we stopped at a street corner and all three of us got out.

Then, with the taxi driver and myself acting as her body guards, Supin simply began to give out the money she had won at the casino to the poor kids on the street.

To begin with all the kids were happy and shouting. But then other people began to join in and the crowd grew rapidly and the mood started to darken. In the end a group of angry men were fighting to get toward us and we were in danger of being swamped so we had to get back in the taxi and drive off quickly.

The taxi driver refused to say anything on the way back. It was obvious he was furious. We gave him a good tip but he didn't thank us. But as were going into the hotel lobby Supin turned to me and said, 'I sure we done the right thing. We got to help people if we can.'

A picture I took of this strange event is on the desk in front of me now. There she is! Handing out her largesse with such a practised ease! The crowd must have thought she was some mad member of the Thai Royal Family.

There were people who criticised Supin. They said it was an act of vanity but I disagreed. It was typical of Supin. It was impulsive, it certainly wasn't thought out, but to me it showed a proper generosity of spirit.

After that we hired a car and drove down to the country to visit her brother who had a small farm in Prachinburi.

I played with the children and looked around the farm while she talked family business with her brother. In the end she gave him a good sum of money so that he could buy more land but I never got the full detail. Overall I don't think it was very satisfactory because when we returned to England it was never mentioned again.

There were other occasions, when we had smaller wins, that we went on holidays that were more modest.

On one occasion after she had won a few hundred pounds she said she wanted to visit Scotland. So we spent an uncomfortable weekend in a hotel in the Highlands where the heating didn't work and it rained all the time. Another time we took the Eurostar train to Paris. It came out of the tunnel on the French side with a whoosh. We stayed in a small hotel in Montmartre and sat at pavement cafes and pretended we were French.

Our best holiday was when we went to Holland to see the tulips. For some reason we took George. He had never been abroad before and all the way over he sat looking out of the window of the plane.

George talked a lot about the time during the war when he had been evacuated as a child from Liverpool to stay with a family in Wales. He said that was the only time he'd ever experienced any real family life. I think that was why George liked being with us. We became a sort of family to him.

Supin was more comfortable in a wheelchair then. So I am at the far side of one the tulip fields. I am watching old George, with his long face and his Liverpool accent, pushing Supin. They have stopped for a moment to look at the mauve carpet of tulips in front of them. They are both wrapped up in coats as the day has turned cold.

Then George leans forward and says something to Supin which makes her laugh and then he is pushing her on once more.

When I look back now, as I write this account, I realise that those two had something special about them. They were both outsiders, both gamblers, but to my way of thinking they also had a proper humanity, a real richness, about them.

## 11

The Bluffer was a Tory through and through.

You could put up a hat stand for election and providing the hat on it was blue the Bluffer would vote for it and swear all our troubles were over. On one occasion when we were in Wales and still had the factory he took my mother and Ida ( my mother's maiden aunt) up to Dolgellau in the old Triumph 2000 to hear Selwyn Lloyd speak. He came back glowing with enthusiasm. But he also thought Enoch Powell had it about right. So when the Ugandan Asians came over in 1968 and the government asked people to lodge them he said, 'That's all very well but once you get the buggers in you'll never get them out.'

But there is a certain type of Tory who is also an adventurer and who believes the game's the thing. He's still a patriot, still believes that twenty shillings make a pound and that England is the best nation in the world. But at the same time he has some secret itch to turn over the tables and create a bit of mayhem.

All countries have them. The French have Antoine de Saint-Exupery. Before the war he and his fellow aviators flew down the coast of Africa in primitive planes and then crossed the Atlantic to South America to set up a postal service. Over the years a lot of them died when their planes went down.

During his twenty years in the clothing trade the Bluffer had conformed. He had bitten his lip and played the game, buttering up to the buyers at the big stores.

But now he was out. His days in the factory were over. Once again he was a free man.

When it was established that the coast was clear smuggling operations were resumed and it became obvious, unless the people of the West Midlands had an insatiable thirst for Spanish brandy, that the Bluffer had widened his horizons and was bringing in other goods.

His favourite film was The Third Man though I doubt if he was smuggling penicillin. But then again with the Bluffer you never knew.

Certainly by this time he had established a reputation in the Birmingham area. It was the period in the late 1960s before customs barriers came down in Europe and there was a market for all sorts of smuggled goods.

At one point he was even talking about bringing in carpets.

But my mother was pressing for an end to operations. Debts had been paid off and there was enough money to begin the conversion. She was also probably more aware than the Bluffer of the danger they were in.

A compromise was reached. They agreed three or four more shiploads and then he would wrap it up.

There are people who have a nose for when something is not right. George Lynes was like that. He could look around and tell you straight away if there was a scam being played out on one of the tables.

In the end Supin was the same. She would never play on a table where she did not feel comfortable.

The Bluffer also had the same nose for danger.

On the night of the last smuggling operation Bronwen is in the car on the front at Aberdyfi as usual.

She has just flashed out the all clear and the boat, with Bert at the tiller and the Bluffer and Tug Roberts amidships, is heading out into the open sea for the rendezvous with the Spanish trawler.

Then slowly the Bluffer looks around. His face is up. It is almost as if he is sniffing the wind. I have seen him do that before. He has sensed something. He doesn't hesitate. He just turns to Bert and says quietly, ' I think we'll just turn it around tonight Bert. Call it a night.'

And that is what happened. The Bluffer was in charge. Nobody argued. They turned back to Aberdyfi and made the prearranged sign to Bronwen in the car that the mission had been aborted. They are about to tie her up in Aberdyfi when he turns to Bert and says with a little smile on the corner of his lips, 'Take her on up the river Bert my boy, let's see what happens.'

And off they set, the Bluffer humming a little tune as they go. Maybe it was the Bluffer's exceptional antennae for danger telling him that something was not right. Or maybe he'd had a whisper that we had been betrayed, that someone on our team had made a phone call they shouldn't have.

They tied up at the boathouse an hour later. They had motored up. No need to worry about making a noise. When they land the Bluffer turns to the customs officer waiting on the lawn and says, cool as a cucumber, ' Nice evening for a sail sir.'

It was after that, when the customs officer had inspected the boat and gone away empty handed, that my Mother sat the Bluffer down and informed him officially that his days as a smuggler were over.

But they had done very well out of it. When they took the money out of the safe and counted it all up they were astonished at how much they had made.

But they still ceased all criminal activities. They resumed their role as upright citizens. They gave drinks parties and mixed with the local gentry. When he had been in the clothing trade the Bluffer and my mother had twice been invited to garden parties at Buckingham Palace with the Queen so they knew how to behave in that sort of society.

During that winter Llugwy Hall was given a face lift. The place buzzed with carpenters and brick layers and plumbers and electricians. The Bluffer as well as being the paymaster is also chief architect and foreman. His word is law. One minute he is up a ladder worrying about guttering and the next he is telling the electricians to make sure they give him enough power to run the kitchen. He is there shouting heave ho late one afternoon when they remove the last bricks and open up the old cellar.

He is on his own. This is his project. He has never been so happy.

We know we are approaching the end when one day Terry Platt the wine merchant arrives. Cases of wine are brought inside and over lunch a wine list is drawn up and priced.

The Bluffer organises the hotel in the way he wants. The core staff, those judged to be loyal, are drawn from the brandy smuggling gang. He runs the hotel like one of his irregular war time units. Cash in hand, notes in back pocket, not a word. Loyalty and discretion rewarded. We are a team, all in on the act.

But my mother, God bless her, is the real hero of this period in their lives. She will later become a painter of some talent. She will hold her own exhibitions.

But when she was young, she had been an only child, she had developed a way with animals.

The summer prior to the hotel opening a local farmer gave her a fox cub he had rescued. It lived with them all that summer running up and down the lawn in the evenings.

My mother's greatest pleasure was to walk along the river bank and then up into the hills behind. This is in fact where we scattered her ashes. But now she is thrust into the maelstrom of a working kitchen. Not just in it. She must take charge of it.

While the Bluffer is out at the front showing off to his guests she must maintain the boiler room of the operation.

But she does it. Because she is cut from the same cloth as the Bluffer. Stand up straight. Don't complain. Get on with the job.

But the worry of it takes its toll. For a week before they open that Easter she takes to her bed with nerves.

The Bluffer operates front of house. He treats his customers like his friends, which a lot of them become.

The Bluffer is always innovative, always forward thinking.

He buys tins, in commercial size quantities, of what are called ‘ exotic salads’ from an address on the Mile End Road. They are put on the train at Paddington and picked up at Machynlleth. He orders Guinea Fowl in tins from Alveston Kitchens in Warwickshire. I suppose they must have come by train as well. I know all this because he told me.

The Bluffer also says we were the first hotel in Mid Wales to use a micro wave oven. Can that be right? How can he know that? Anyway whatever it was we had done we were proud of it. The Bluffer bought the microwave after attending a trade show in London and it sat proudly in a corner of the kitchen.

As the guests in the dining room look out over the River Dyfi, one of the best trout rivers in Wales, they compliment the kitchen on the quality of the trout.

They are of course unaware that the trout comes frozen in a box marked Japan and has been defrosted in our microwave. The point the Bluffer made years later, when he was challenged about this, was that if the guests enjoyed their trout what difference did it make where it came from?

Was a trout not a trout whether it came from Wales or Japan or Timbuctoo?

No one knew how to answer that.

As he got older, as we all do, the Bluffer started to repeat himself.

When he was describing, as he did, the workings of the kitchen he always concluded by saying sharply, ‘Of course we never served steak. We didn’t know how to do that.’

Then he would looked around the room to see if anyone might challenge this odd assertion.

Going through the Bluffer’s papers I found all the old menus and tariff sheets and prospectuses. I even found an old guest book and thumbing through it I was able to put faces to many of the names. A lot of them came from the Birmingham area, they owned small businesses there. Some of them went out and stood on the lawn with the Bluffer and I could see he was indicating things to them so I guessed that some of them might have been his clients from when, as he described it, he was in the ' brandy trade.'

But in the years they ran the hotel the Bluffer and my mother worked their socks off. The Bluffer took round early morning teas and newspapers and then sat up till one the next morning with the last sorry toper. My mother never deserted her post in the kitchen. They worked hard. They were not shirkers. They were of that generation.

When they looked back later they both said it had been one of the best times of their lives. And now I have scattered both their ashes on the hill up behind the hotel.

# 12

The thick manila envelope, and beside it the faded red folder that contained the manuscript of Counterpart, lay unopened on the desk for most of the morning. Instead I mooched around doing other things.

I spent time outside inspecting his vegetable garden and then in a drawer I found his passport and an old wallet and a watch and a pair of cufflinks.

After lunch I took several boxes of books to the charity shop.

There are always surprises when you clear out an old man's home.

Whenever there was a funeral or a wedding or a church service to attend he always said, 'Well I had better put on the old blue suit,' and there was always a joke about whether it would last him out or not. But when I went through his effects I found there were three blue suits all slightly different.

I put the file containing Counterpart to one side and open up the manila envelope.

To my astonishment I discover that several years ago The Bluffer had put a private detective on me. The envelope contains his report. The private detective appears to be a former contact who once worked for military intelligence in Belfast.

There is no easy way to get all the elements of this story down in the correct order because the way they tumbled out was, like life, quite haphazard. To make them more ' comprehensible' would be to skew what was happening.

In 1972 when I was twenty two years old and the Bluffer and my Mother were still living in Wales and running the hotel, and long before I married Supin, I emigrated to Canada and after a while got a job working for the Truro Daily News in Nova Scotia.

Peter Duffy was my boss and Don Retson was my co reporter. Jerry Simons was our news editor, he took over from Peter Harris. I recall one evening when it began to snow that Jerry went out for a walk. When he came back he sat down and returned to his work not knowing that he had an inch of snow on top of his head. I heard later that he went out West but there was some problem with an underage girl and he ended up in jail. Incidentally many years later I wrote to Duffy and regaled him with some of the things we got up to then but he replied back that he had no recollection of me at all. Anyhow in the spring of 1974 I decided to leave my job in Truro and go down to Mexico.

I took a plane to Boston. Then one evening, I recall how red the sun was as it was going down, I walked out of the town to begin hitching lifts down to the south. I didn't mind where I slept in those days. I had taken it into my mind that I would go to Veracruz. Perhaps I thought I was going to meet someone called Veracruz. Those sorts of detail have gone the way of all memory. I was in a car travelling south when the driver said he was pulling into Savannah, Georgia for the night. It was raining so the alternative was sitting up all night in a gas station. He dropped me off at a motel and I counted up how much money I had left and discovered it was not a lot.

I telephoned the editor of the daily paper, the Savannah Morning News, and said I was a hot shot reporter looking for a job and he replied that he had a vacancy for a copy editor on the rim, so I said I would take that.

My memories of Savannah are mostly good. I recall when Ronnie Thompson, known as Machine Gun Ronnie, was standing for Governor of Georgia. He came into the news room to solicit our votes and shake our hands. His campaign buttonhole was a tiny silver machine gun. There are other evenings, again it seems to be election time, spent drinking in Pinkie Master's saloon.

I have checked on Wikipedia and apparently it was in Pinkie Master's that Jimmy Carter got up on a table and announced that he would run for president.

But that summer we talked about another president, Richard Nixon.

I had a black and white television in my room on which I watched all the impeachment hearings.

I was in the news room the night he resigned. As soon as I heard the bell I ran into the wire room and ripped off the flash from the AP teleprinter – Nixon Resigns. I know that is not much of a souvenir for a life time as a reporter. Somehow I have always managed to be several steps away from the action. I should have kept the machine gun replica, it would have been a more interesting talking point. But that is the way it is.

That makes me stop for a moment. Someday my children will go through my papers in the same way that I am going through the Bluffer's. They will certainly come across that faded piece of wire copy and have no idea of its significance. Had I better explain before it is too late?

Another evening I was in the composing room, supervising the pasting up of a story, it was an article about the Ku Klux Klan and I said something that was not very complimentary about the Klan and one of the paste up girls said, 'You'd better watch out mister one of the guys over there is a leading light.'

I stayed six months in Savannah before heading back up North to Canada.

# 13

The file is headed Report of Private Detective. The name of the gumshoe has been blotted out with a thick black marker pen.

I hesitated for a long time before starting to read it.

I have often thought how different my life would have been if I hadn't taken the ride into Savannah that night. I could have stayed out on the road, spent the night in the gas station and continued on in the morning toward Veracruz in Mexico.

In fact in the last few years it was something that had come to obsess me. I began to study maps of Mexico and Veracruz on the internet. I went as far as checking out airline possibilities for getting there.

When I looked at the private detective's report I saw that The Bluffer had been following the same trail.

I squeezed up my eyes. I was trying to recollect if I had told the Bluffer about taking that ride into Savannah. But nothing came. But I must have said something. The Bluffer never forgot anything. He would had tucked the information away for when he needed it.

In the same way that I do, he also wants to find out how my life would have turned out if I had continued on to Veracruz rather than stopping in Savannah.

I read the opening pages and then pushed back my chair and looked out of the window for a long time. From where I was sitting I could see the Bluffer's vegetable garden. Towards the end he had devised a system of raised beds so he would not have to bend. I can see him standing there digging leeks or whatever it was he did. He would have been wearing that old blue sleeveless sweater. He had a habit every so often, like an animal almost, of raising his head and sniffing the wind before continuing.

The private detective, based in Belfast, has sub contracted the job to an agency in Mexcio City and they have sent a man down to Veracruz. It's a fat file, almost a hundred pages. I look out of the window again. I'll bet that cost a pretty penny. To his credit the Bluffer, who always makes a joke about his supposed meanness with money, will spend when it's necessary. But he is of that war time generation and he doesn't like waste. There are a lot of people like that. How many today are aware that in France the population was rationed to twelve hundred calories a day during the German occupation and the incidence of diabetes died away completely? There are advantages.

The report states that a young man arrived by train at the railway station in Veracruz on a pleasant evening in May 1974. He took a room in a cheap hotel behind the station. Here for some reason he seems to have stopped using the name Rorie Smith. He signs the register as Arthur Polianski, a name he continues to use from then on.

He stays at the same hotel for two weeks while he familiarises himself with the city. Then when he has the lie of the land, he rents a small apartment on a narrow street near the waterfront where he stays for two years.

Our gumshoe has been very thorough. He has gone to the apartment and interviewed the landlord, who is still there. He says that of course he remembers Polianski. He says occasionally he used to bring girls back to the apartment and sometimes there were parties, but on the whole he was no trouble.

According to the report it was two years before Polianski's Spanish was good enough for him to function properly.

But during that learning period his time wasn't wasted. He got a job as a runner with a local news agency. He picked up parcels from the station and delivered messages.

When he could more or less function in the language he was allowed to go down to the police station to question officers over the details of cases. They paid him only enough to live on, but he didn't mind, he was learning.

He spent his evenings in the dives and the bars of the Veracruz water front. A lot of the rougher bars are gone now but the gumshoe has managed to find some people who still recall him. He is described as, ' Quite large and friendly but occasionally useful with his fists.' The Belfast private detective has added his own note querying as to whether that translation is accurate. The Bluffer has added an exclamation mark and then pencilled in beside it, ' Sounds like Mac from the old days.'

Polianski got his break when he came under the tutelage of a man called Hubert Schleck who had worked as a sports reporter for the Miami Herald. Hubert knew everything there was to know about baseball but he was fired after he got into a fight with a desk man who had come home at the wrong time to find Hubert in bed with his wife. In the fight that followed Hubert had bitten half his ear off. If it had just been a tussle then it might have been overlooked but when the desk man appeared for work with his ear all bandaged up so that he looked like Vincent van Gogh the editor said it was intolerable and Hubert had to go. So now he ran a news agency in Veracruz, scraping a living sending stories up to the big dailies in Mexico City. As an apprenticeship for Polianski it could not have been bettered.

Soon he knew all the policemen in the area and his nights in the waterfront dives also gave him a good network of contacts.

According to the report there were nights when he didn't go to bed at all. He would emerge from a bar as the sun was rising and go out to a spot he knew where he could take an early morning dip to freshen up. Then he would eat a good breakfast at a waterfront cafe before reporting for work at Hubert's agency.

His first bylined piece, which appeared in all the national papers, was the story of the Veracruz fisherman who brought in the biggest shark that had been seen on the coast for years. But when it was cut open the half digested remains of a four year old boy were found inside. Polianski had been on the spot when the boat came in. He always carried a camera with him so he got the pictures as well. Hubert gave him a small rise after that.

It was about this time, the gumshoes's report states, and the Bluffer has heavily underlined this passage, that Polinaski took up with a young woman called Carmen Martinez, a dancer at one of the bars. Soon they were being seen around together. The gumshoe describes them as being an ' item.'

Certainly Polianski seems to have picked well because years later they are still together.

After four years with Hubert Schleck, Polianski is talent spotted by a national outfit and because of his dual language ability is made use of in an international context. He makes his name reporting on the turbulence in Chile and Argentina. He shows himself to be fearless in pursuit of a story and comes under fire several times. After that he does a stint in Europe living for a couple of years in Madrid. Then there is a year in London covering for a correspondent on long term leave.

The Bluffer has underlined the passage where it says that Polianski and Carmen took a two week holiday in Devon and Cornwall staying at bed and breakfasts and swimming every day.

The Bluffer has added a note in the margin. 'I wonder if they bathed at Beer?'

After they return home from Europe there is something of a hiatus in the life of Carmen and

Polianski. Even the Mexico City gumshoe says it is unclear why he parted company with his employers. There is some speculation. He had been working very hard, so maybe he was burned out. There was also a report that he had been drinking too much. But the most likely hypothesis, the gumshoe writes, is that he fell out with an editor over a minor detail and it escalated.

It is here that Polianski makes one of the few misjudgements of his life in Mexico. He has decided to leave journalism and open a restaurant. They also now have a child, he is called Felix. Carmen is also anxious to return to Veracruz to be near her family.

( I am rather summarising the report here, which is lengthy and includes a lot of extraneous detail about their daily lives at that time).

The gumshoe reports them as scouting properties on the sea front. Then three months later they have bought into a rundown restaurant and are doing it up. But right from the start they are undercapitalised.

No doubt there has been some severance pay from Polianski's job but the life of a foreign correspondent is not conducive to making savings.

In the margin of the report, in his rather school boy hand, the Bluffer has noted, ' Usual problem. Insufficient capital. Probably had to borrow from family. Why did they not get in touch?'

At the start all goes well. Polianski is known in the town and Carmen also has her contacts. The staff come mostly from her family.

But in a year the first cracks begin to show. The initial momentum cannot be kept up. Bills are going unpaid and Polianski is looking increasingly worried. Then suddenly it is over. The closed sign goes up and Carmen and Polianski and young Felix move out. It is a very bad moment for them.

The gumshoe has noted, 'Capital exhausted' and The Bluffer has added an exclamation mark in pencil. They take a small apartment only a couple of blocks from the cheap hotel where Polianski first stayed when he arrived in Veracruz ten years before. Carmen's younger sister moves in with them to look after Felix while Carmen takes a job as a waitress.

This is a period when Polianski does a lot of mooching. He walks the length of the seafront. When the weather is favourable he goes swimming. He spends long nights in the clubs and bars. Hubert Schleck has gone back to Miami but he picks up with other friends and contacts from the old days.

After three months Carmen confronts him and the situation is brought to a head. Then all the bottles are thrown out and the apartment is swept clean.

The Bluffer has noted in the margin, ' Very short of cash.'

Then one morning Polianski takes a table and chair out on to the roof terrace of the apartment and sits down to write an article for a magazine about his experiences as a foreign correspondent.

On the strength of half a dozen pieces they give up the small apartment and take a larger place with a balcony over looking the sea. And it is there that Polianski begins his second career as a novelist.

Some of the critics on the literary magazines accuse him of trying to write like Hemingway but his publishers continue to back him. The sales for the first two books are slow. But the third book is *Tombola!* the story of a diabolical newspaper magnate, and it sells well. After that there is a book every couple of years.

This is where the report concludes. At the end the Bluffer has written 'Very Satisfactory!' and put a thick pencil tick by the side of it.

# 14

When I had finished reading the Report of the Private Detective on the life of my fictional nemesis Arthur Polianski I looked up to see that it was dark outside. I closed the file and went outside.

The moon was out and a cold wind was blowing through the trees.

I listened for an age for any word from Supin, or my mother or Alison or even the Bluffer.

But all I could hear was the noise of the wind. Eventually I was driven back inside by the cold.

Logs were stacked up in the porch so I lit a fire and made myself a plate of scrambled eggs on toast. Then I went to the drinks cupboard and brought out a bottle of Jamesons. The Bluffer hasn't touched anything but Jamesons for years now. I filled a jug of water and put in on a table. Then I drew up one of the armchairs to the fire. In the drinks cupboard I had discovered a packet of small cigars.

I started to work my way through the bottle of whiskey. Every so often I lit a cigar. I brooded and stared into the fire. I went over old ground and saw where wrong turns had been taken. There were battles that should have been joined that had been skirted around. There were other lives that could have been led.

The morning light found me slumped asleep in the chair. I got up, showered and ate a good breakfast. Then I poured the dregs of the whiskey down the sink and cleared out the ashtray and went for a walk in the fresh morning air.

And that is how those ghosts were exorcised.

# 15

A month after we got back from the holiday in Thailand where Supin had handed out the money to the poor children in Khlong Toei I asked for a meeting with John Gibson at Derriford Hospital in Plymouth.

This was because Supin's physical condition was deteriorating.

She was now locked up and stiff for hours at a time. This was frustrating for her as she had to wait for the tablets to do their work before she could move again. Her mood swings also became more exaggerated. This made family life increasingly uneasy.

She was also having difficulty with her balance and was now walking with a stick. Shortly she would find it easier to use a frame and then a wheelchair.

We went to see our GP who prescribed anti depressants but she had to give them up when they reacted badly with the Parkinson's drugs.

Then at the hospital John Gibson explained that the disease could stay stable for long periods before a sudden alteration. However the good news he was able to give us was that we were moving up the list for the Deep Brain Stimulation operation. At that time, for our region, only Steven Gill of Frenchay Hospital in Bristol was doing the operation, so we had to wait our turn.

John Gibson then increased the dosage of the Sinemet and wished us well. He was a kind man and doing the best he could, but it was not an easy battle for him either. He knew as well as we did that while the Sinemet would certainly free her up, it would also cause an increase in the main side effect, the involuntary muscle movements called dyskinesia, which made her twitch and jerk.

In my opinion it was this advance of the disease, and the higher dosage of medication, that began to affect Supin's judgement as a gambler.

The discipline she had shown before was now missing and she began to lose heavily.

It was George who gave me the detail. She had lost one evening and against his advice had borrowed a thousand pounds from a Chinese man. This man was outside our circle and had a very bad reputation. In other words my wife was suddenly in serious trouble.

It was at this moment that Ivor Dryer entered our lives.

Ivor was a small man with dark curly hair and I disliked him straightaway. He had a business filming the races at some of the smaller meetings such as Newton Abbot and Exeter. But in the casino he operated as a money lender. And that as we were all about to find out was a dangerous business.

But at the time he offered a solution to our problems. Mr Chong had warned us that failure to keep up the repayments to the Chinese man would have serious consequences. So when Ivor offered to pay the Chinese man off and to loan Supin the money himself on more affordable terms she accepted.

Normally gamblers are very clever when they go looking for funds.

For the crucial period, Lazarus like, they are able to dispense with sticks and rise from wheelchairs, at the same rediscovering the full power of speech, as they make their way into the bank to arrange an overdraft or a small loan.

But on this occasion the amount she needed was just too big. It was also a time when I was beginning to dig in my heels.

So this became a difficult moment for us. Supin was angry and frustrated with me. She saw my unwillingness to fund her properly as the reason she was in trouble now. I found myself thinking of the Bluffer and how all those years ago his clothing business in Wales had also failed because it was under capitalised.

In the end the situation took a turn that was completely unexpected.

This was because Ivor was not as good a money lender as he thought he was. He had lent money to people who had not repaid him and soon he was in trouble himself.

Then one evening we are at home. George is with us as well. We are sitting in the conservatory looking out over the garden. Funds to gamble have dried up almost completely. It is George who makes the announcement. He glances at Supin, gives a little cough and then turns to me and says in his thick Liverpool accent, but rather awkwardly, as if he does not quite believe it himself:

'Ivor says we ought to rob the casino. That's the way we get our money back.'

I stared at them in astonishment. I could not believe what I was hearing. I waited for someone to say it was a joke but no laugh came. Supin was staring hard at me, calibrating my reaction. Then they gave me the details. Ivor was to be our organiser. Mr Chong would be our armourer. With his connections he could supply Ivor with a gun. Jackie was in on it as well as he knew where all the alarms and security cameras were situated and how to disable them. George and Supin would be in the raiding party. I had been volunteered to drive the getaway car.

Of course I refused point blank.

'It's the stupidest thing I had ever heard of in my life,' I said angrily. 'We have more chance of flying to the moon than successfully robbing the casino. It will certainly end with us all being jailed, deservedly, for very long periods.'

I kept up this vigorous attack over the next few days. I wanted to ram home the point and stop any crazy planning before it got started.

We could certainly have used the money. I also surprised myself when I realised that I would have had few scruples in robbing the gangsters who ran the casino if I thought we could get away with it. But with our hobbledehoy group we stood no chance.

My rejection of the plan only made Supin more angry and frustrated. She became convinced that I was thwarting what she saw as the best way of resolving her financial troubles. At this point there was no doubt that her judgement was becoming terribly clouded by the Parkinson's disease and the medication she was taking.

A month after George has made his announcement we are at home one evening. We have just finished eating.

This is a time when Supin doesn't look well at all. One of her eyelids has started to droop and her speech is beginning to blur. The meal has been eaten largely in silence.

I knew something was going to happen when she pushed her plate to one side and reached down to her handbag which was on the floor by her chair.

She lifted it up onto the table and began to rumble about in the bottom.

Then, with an angry heave, she pulled out a large pistol. She held it in her hand for a moment and looked straight at me. Then she put it down on the table in front of her with a hard clunk.

I didn't say anything. I was too surprised to open my mouth. But her words when they came out were crystal clear.

' Ivor says I going to carry the gun. We going to do it. So you either in or out.'

# 16

So what was my part in this whole mad farrago?

It was, to my great and eternal shame, to absent myself from it as often as I could. That is not to say I did not love them both dearly.

If the Bluffer had said, 'Look old boy, been drinking too much, kidney packed up, any chance you can help out?' I would have offered myself for a transplant the same day.

Similarly if the doctors had declared that it was possible for me to share my store of dopamine with Supin, again I would have volunteered with a light heart.

But I don't have the fund of war stories that the Bluffer has. Neither have I been a gambler. I also cannot paint and I have never planted a tree.

So in the end my sole contribution to this particular game has been to place one foot after another, rather in the manner of an insensible beast.

But I covered the distance. Even my sternest critics would give me credit for that.

It should also be stated that the events described in this book took place over a period of about thirty years. So there were times when I could be away.

So one night at home I opened up an old school atlas at a double page of Europe. Then in pencil and using a ruler I drew a line across from West to East. Porto to Istanbul. I didn't discuss it with anyone else. I might as well have sat down and said, 'Well I am going to go to the Moon, what does anyone think about that?'

When I did set off I made all the normal sort of arrangements. Monies were allocated, cleaners, carers, friends, family were all detailed to come in. But I was still accused of deserting my post, of running away from the battle.

My justification was, 'If I am shovelled into my grave before you two what good am I then?'

However this is a defense that even now is not accepted by some of my critics. It was also a defense that was not accepted by Supin, who was very critical of my actions. I was expected, like a loyal captain, to stay at my post and go down with my ship.

But I didn't.

Instead I walked across plains, I walked up hills, I crossed countries. By the time I had finished I had walked across Europe. And when I had done that I started to train so I could swim the Hellespont and escape into Asia.

But when you have two powerful people, in the form of the Bluffer and Supin, who are both after your hide you have to keep going. Because if you fall they will be on your neck and that will be the end of everything.

Most of the appellations for what I have done, backpacker, rambler, hiker, even walker, do not really fit. I like the word routard. It may not be exact, but it has the right sound. Somebody of the road, the route. I have been over hill and down dale and the converse and I have on occasion found myself unwillingly in industrial zones and on the edge of motorways. But a steady pace along a quiet D road seems to do the trick for me.

It all began when I was working for Television South West in Plymouth.

My title, investigative journalist, was painted on the frosted glass of my office door. My bosses were Michael Reinhold and Ken Seymour. Occasionally some one would push a jokey note under the door telling me to investigate the men's toilet that was not flushing properly but aside from that I was left pretty much alone. I nosed around, much in the way the Bluffer might have done. I would meet a private detective called Jack Haddon in the bar of the Walrus and give him twenty pounds and he would give me some piece of information. Then I would go back to my office and type up a report on it and file it and that kept everyone happy.

This was a calm and happy period in our lives. It was several years before the diagnosis of Parkinson's. The children were growing up contentedly. Supin was gardening and cooking and enjoying her carpentry. She made a whole set of kitchen cupboards in a month. Most days I would go home for lunch parking the company car with the Television South West logo on it outside the front door.

Actually I did unearth one story. I discovered that Shams Badram, a former Egyptian Minister of War who had been sentenced, in absentia, to thirty years in jail by a court in Cairo on charges of torturing political opponents to death, was now, under light cover, running a feta cheese factory in Okehampton. But as he moved in the same social circles as the directors of Television South West the story was never broadcast and my moment of glory was denied.

That was the high point of my time in the world of television. After that it was discovered that I was investigating the mysterious flight of Rudolf Hess to Britain in 1941. The official story was that Hess was on a peace mission but a doctor in South Wales was convinced that it was not Hess who had made the flight but a double. When it was discovered that I was planning to write a book about it that was the finish and I had to go. It was put around that my nerves had got the better of me.

They sent me to see a man called Nigel Giggs. I have tried to check him out on Google and Wikipedia but I can find no trace of him. Today he would be called a counsellor but my mother would probably would have referred to him as a ' nerve man.' In face he was an ex soldier. I went to his office one day and he had a map spread out on the table. He said, 'I want you to walk twenty miles along the coastal path from Salcombe to Dartmouth.'

So the following week that is what I did, going via Hallsands, Slapton and Stoke Fleming. Afterwards I never felt better. So that is how I learned about walking. All this is true.

## 17

The life of a routard is an easy one. Rise from roadside encampment or cheap hotel, walk, eat, sleep, shit, find further lodging for night. It is also a good life for a writer. The words get hammered out with the pace of the stride.

I had crossed Portugal, not without some misadventures, almost being run down several times on its narrow roads. Spain was easier. I crossed the border at Miranda do Douro then went up to Zamora, Valladolid and Palencia. I walked beside the Canal de Castilla in the autumn when the leaves were turning golden and a sharp wind was beginning to blow. But the days were still sunny. I have a great memory of those days. Then it is Burgos, Logrono, Pamplona and Jaca. I arrived in Jaca in time for Christmas and crossed the Col du Somport in the snow into France. The regions of the Bearn and Gers are fine and delicate but the season had turned once again by the time I reached Montpelier and I recall collapsing on the bed of a cheap hotel overcome with exhaustion. In Arles I thought of Vincent van Gogh. Then it was up to Les Baux de Provence, and then along to Saint Remy de Provence and then on toward Cavaillon, Apt and Manosque. Is there anywhere more unpleasant than the hinterland of the Cote d'Azur? Then crossing the River Var and a last long day before finally arriving at Menton. The next stop is Ventimigilia and Italy.

I was approaching Capo Noli on the Italian Riviera one evening and casting about for a place to put up my tent when I looked over my shoulder and saw a man coming up behind me. When he came closer I could see that he had a rucksack on his back. Then he dumped the bag down beside me and we shook hands and this was my introduction to Vilis Balodis, hailing originally from the port city of Liepaja but late resident of the Latvian capital city of Riga.

A hundred metres further on there was a small beach. We clambered down to it and seeing a piece of dry land above the tide mark pitched our tents. We collected sticks off the beach and lit a fire and pooled our resources which came to a loaf of bread, two tins of tuna, two oranges, a bar of chocolate and most importantly a bottle of wine, almost full.

It is very rare to meet another routard on the road these days so it was a special treat to spend that evening with Vilis.

We swapped our stories. Vilis was far more of a routard than I. (In truth I was really quite a fraud. I could have given up any time and bought a ticket home. I don't think Vilis could). He was small and wore rather battered glasses. His hair was cut short. His clothes were shabby and seemed to be coated with a film of dust.

He told me he had spent a year studying in England but now he was a painter, on his way to Rome to make his name. However as he was not in any hurry he preferred to walk rather than go by train or bus. When we had finished eating we rolled cigarettes. He had been on the road a lot longer than me. For the first leg of his journey he had gone to Paris where he had spent several months and then he had descended down through Switzerland to reach the coast at Menton. He said he was fed up with mountains and wanted to walk by the sea. He must have been just behind me all the way up the coast, slowly catching me up.

We talked until the fire began to die and the last of the wine was finished. We agreed that we would meet up again in a few days time at the Hotel Bologna in Genoa.

The next morning Vilis was up before me and soon he had disappeared into the distance. By now I was looking forward to arriving in Genoa. My experience of the aging Italians on this Riviera coast had been discouraging. They looked soft, lying on their sun loungers, drinking coffee, eating ice creams, occasionally venturing up to their waists in the sea. They were all perfectly bronzed, perfectly wrinkled and in truth, to me, perfectly infantile.

After a while that feeling of ennui that can overtake a routard descended on me once again so I was glad several mornings later when I could look along the coastline and see in the distance the outline of the port buildings of Genoa.

There is another difference between a routard and other walkers that I would like to make. A hiker or a rambler is generally out for a good day in the country but a routard is more intent on getting from point A to point B. Where I could I walked but for instance on entering or leaving cities I often took a local bus or a train.

But this narrative is not intended to be a memoir of a trip, a hike, a walk, an adventure. Perhaps I will write that another day. Any good book shop has shelves lined with books that cover the subject. The obvious starting places are with W.H. Davies and Laurie Lee. But there are some accounts which are lamentable. I saw the other day that a man has written a book about carrying a fridge around Ireland.

I had great difficulty in Portugal because I had decided to follow the River Douro going East. There were no footpaths and only one narrow road. On several occasions I was almost knocked down by heavy trucks. I have nothing against the Portuguese. I slept in their orange groves, ate their good cod fish, and admired the fine city of Porto and wished that I could take an evening cruise on the beautiful River Douro. But I could not continue on foot. So half way across I took a bus to the Spanish border and started again.

Later when I arrived on the Adriatic coast of Italy I could not face the further tramp around to Trieste and down the long Croatian coast. So I started again in Dubrovnik. I wish now that I had walked the Italian

Adriatic coast, however dull it is, down to Bari and caught the boat over to Dubrovnik from there.

The total distance that I walked across Europe I estimated at about two and a half thousand miles.

Finally I arrived in the industrial zone of Genoa and took the commuter train into the city and met up once again with Vilis at the Hotel Bologna. He had pushed himself at a pace and arrived two days before me.

I was pleased to see him again, company is important to a routard. We drank beer and ate delicious homemade hamburgers in a crowded restaurant in the Via de Pre and afterwards sipped coffee and smoked cigarettes in a cafe by the port.

Vilis explained that as well as being an artist he also saw himself as a revolutionary. His view was that the artist who did not want to overturn the established order of things was not a real artist at all. He was well read and could quote the poet Shelley at length. He also knew the writings of Tom Paine and understood his part in the French and American revolutions. He said those were the sort of people we should admire.

As we walked around the harbour looking at boats and eating ice creams he said he was going to Rome, partly because he was sure he could prosper there as a painter, but also to visit Shelley's grave.

When we had found a bar with a comfortable terrace and sat down and ordered brandies, I paid if I recollect, he began to recite passages from Shelley's famous poem the Mask of Anarchy, even rising to his feet to deliver the well known last stanza with its final line, Ye are Many, They are Few.

When he had finished there was an uneasy pause, other customers in the bar were starting to look at us, and he sat down.

I was truly glad to have met Vilis. It was great to have someone to talk to, especially a fellow routard, but I did not have his learning, or his political fire, and I was beginning to find him a bit of a puzzle.

I filled the gap that followed by asking the waiter to bring us more brandies. Then there was a further long pause. I sensed there was something more he wanted to say. We both lit cigarettes and I waited. I could see him hesitating but then he appeared to change his mind and he got up and said we had drunk too much and we should clear our heads.

So after that we climbed up the streets at the back of the harbour until we could get a good view down onto the bay. From there we watched the ferries and the cargo ships and the cruise ships going in and out of the port. Vilis called the cruise ships Pig Boats. He said they were out of proportion and disgusted him. Then I looked back down the coast to the West to see if I could make out the faint line of Capo Noli, the promontory in the shape of a lion's head, but it was hidden in the haze. Actually it is probably too far away to be seen even on a clear day.

That evening we dined again at the same hamburger restaurant on the Via de Pre. Then after we had made our way back to the hotel and were climbing the stairs to our rooms he said he had something he wanted to show me.

I sat on the bed in his room and he took out a number of his sketch books from his bag. It was obvious that he was a very accomplished artist. The drawings were pen and ink and had nothing at all in common with my mother's paintings. They were of scenes he had observed on the way, with occasional small portraits of people he had persuaded to pose for him, and they were very precise and detailed.

But after what I had heard that afternoon I had been expecting something more expansive and romantic.

When he had closed the last notebook he hesitated for a second, as if he had forgotten something, then he opened up the door to the rickety wardrobe in the corner and took out a thin nylon bag. For a moment I thought it was the bag in which he kept the poles and pegs for his tent. But when he slid the tubes out of the bag and began to assemble them I could see it was something different.

When he had put it all together and drawn back the string, luckily he didn't insert the bolt, I realised that what he had constructed was a sort of homemade crossbow. When I asked him if it was a replica he said certainly not, and that if used correctly it was as good as a gun.

Then he carefully disassembled this bizarre weapon and put it back in its bag.

I did not feel like going to sleep after that so I suggested we go and drink a night cap and so we descended once again into the Via de Pre and found a bar.

He said the world was a pretty filthy sort of place, with all sorts of exploitation and corruption. He said when he had first arrived in England he had planned to assassinate the Queen. He stared at me over the table in the gloomy bar and said he could not understand how a country as modern as England could bear to put up with a monarchy. I replied, by this time we were both drunk, that she was well guarded and that the chances of getting a shot off, even with a crossbow, were minimal.

Our discussions ended when the bar closed and we returned, slightly unsteadily, to our rooms at the Hotel Bologna. I was not used to heavy drinking so when I woke the next morning I had a hangover. I also had a feeling that we had spent an evening and half the night, not to mention my money, Vilis had not contributed at all, pleading artistic poverty, talking complete nonsense.

But when I went down stairs the lady at reception told me Vilis had already left. So I didn't suppose we would meet again. His route was different from mine. He was going down the coast past La Spezia to Rome while I was heading across the Po Valley to Ravenna.

Also I was not in a hurry. In the end I spent two more days in Genoa. I went to an internet cafe and found several e mails from the Bluffer. He never minced his words when he was communicating like that. He said my walk was a complete waste of time. I read several of the messages and then deleted the rest. After that I read several of the web sites to catch up on the news. But when I left the internet cafe I felt fed up and annoyed.

E mail and internet didn't interest Supin. So the next day I made some phone calls and sent some cards and then was on my way again.

# 18

A lesser person would have been defeated by the unrelenting progression of Parkinson's disease. They would have given up and stayed at home and lived under doctor's orders.

Supin went the other way. She knew her time was limited so she started to live round the clock. But nothing was ever organised. Instead her life, now including the bizarre plan to rob the casino, became a chaotic on the hoof improvisation.

All this was completely disastrous for the management of Parkinson's disease. Every time we saw John Gibson or any of the other doctors they stressed the importance of a regular lifestyle.

They told us how important it was to take the tablets at the right times and with the correct combinations of food. A good sleep pattern was also vital.

But Supin was like the Bluffer. She lived life on her own terms. So she simply ignored all that.

For instance after the casino closed up in the early hours a group of them now went night fishing.

It was George who drew the parallel between fishing and gambling.

We were sitting in the restaurant of the casino one evening. Supin was playing Blackjack at a table on the far side of the room.

'It's the same thing,' he said in his thick Liverpool accent. 'Both of them casting out their bait. They'll sit all night hoping to land the big one.'

I looked across the table at him. George was spending more and more time with us. He was starting to regard us as family.

He had a room in his nephew's terraced house in Cattedown. But they hated each other and he spent as little time there as possible. George explained that when his nephew couldn't pay the rent he ordered a fridge or a cooker from a catalogue, this was all a few years ago now, and then when it was delivered sold it to a second hand store for cash.

Supin went into the house once and said it was in a disgusting state.

When the casino closes up in the early hours they all get into their cars and set off for Mutton Cove or Laira Bridge or Phoenix Wharf.

It is all many years ago now and it is a struggle to recall all their names. I know there was Neal, who worked on the door alongside Steven Williams. I think Max went too. George would often go with Supin. She was quite frail at that point and I was glad there was someone with her.

When Supin is on one of these late night fishing expeditions it is likely that she will stay till day break. At other times I have known her to still be there at mid morning.

Then she comes back and cooks up a breakfast and cat naps on the sofa until she is ready to go out again in the evening. At that time she can eat or sleep at any hour of the day.

Her mood can also swing abruptly depending on whether she is locked up with the Parkinson's or whether she has had a loss or a win at the casino.

As I write this I can see both of them now. They are down at Mutton Cove which overlooks the river and is across from the park at Mount Edgecumbe. This is Supin's favourite spot.

The sun is coming up and Supin is casting out her line. George is beside her smoking a cigarette. And under the front seat of the old Mondeo, hidden away in her handbag, is the pistol.

I know it is old, probably even qualifying to be called antique, but both George and Mr Chong have told me that it certainly still works and is very powerful. Supin has refused to discuss it with me. She says if I do not want to take part in the robbery it is none of my business. She carries it in her handbag most of the time. It is unloaded, I found the bullets and hid them in a tin in the garage. But she still likes to carry it with her because it gives her a sense of control when her own powers are waning. Normally she is careful with it. She never takes it out of her handbag in public. At home she keeps it in a drawer in the bedroom, although one time she did lose it and we spent an hour searching for it. Eventually we found it wrapped up in a towel in the bread bin where she had put it for safekeeping.

She thought that was very funny.

When I look back now, many years later, I can see how odd it all was. But at that time it was just part of our life.

There were a lot of people, perhaps they considered they were smarter than she was, who never really understood such a unique and eccentric person.

But the other gamblers at the casino and the people who fished down at Mutton Cove understood Supin perfectly and she took time with them. They were her people, they were outsiders too.

One night when she was at Mutton Cove a gang of lads lowered a stolen car down under the water to hide it from the police. If one of the gang disappeared for a while they used to say he had gone up to the university, meaning he was doing a spell in Dartmoor prison.

Supin said if you spent long enough down at Mutton Cove you saw everything.

If the weather is right she will park up the Mondeo and take out a grill from the back and if a fisherman catches something decent she will cook it up for him.

She will add sauces and spices and everyone will agree when they have finished that it is the tastiest fish they have ever eaten.

Supin loved being at Mutton Cove when the dawn came up. The river is narrow there and the war ships and the submarines, as they come in and out of Plymouth Sound, pass close in to the shore. If the crews are lined up on deck she always waves to them.

A lot of the time the only thing they caught was mackerel. But Supin had a way of cooking it, she fried it up with spices till it was brown and crispy, that even today makes my mouth water. When they were down at Mutton Cove, when the season was right, they put down nets and scooped up bucket loads of whitebait which were also delicious.

Supin was too chaotic, too inconsistent, ever to be a successful businesswoman.

But there were moments, especially when she was waiting for the operation and she was taking more tablets than her body could really stand, when she was inspired.

For example if she caught a sea bass she always took it into Platters restaurant on the Barbican. It was still being run by Rocky at that time, and he would give her twenty pounds for it. This would be her seed corn for the evening in the casino. She was always pleased when she could do that.

Then every autumn, before we finally moved over to Cornwall, we crossed the river by the Torpoint ferry and drove round in the old Mondeo to the park at Mount Edgecumbe. There we filled up a large wicker basket with chestnuts that had fallen from the trees and were lying on the ground. Then on the Saturday we would drive to the car boot sale at Richmond Walk and sell them. We could make a hundred pounds easily, dividing the money between us.

One night at the casino Supin turned her fifty pounds into five hundred pounds and drove into town the next day and bought a microwave oven.

And there it still sits, immense and powerful on the sideboard in our small kitchen, a monument to her ingenuity. When I look at it now I remember the microwave the Bluffer bought for the hotel in Wales all those years before.

After that we went back and pretty well cleared the park out of chestnuts but she was never able to repeat the trick.

But then one evening George approached me in the casino. He looked worried. He said he had been fishing with Supin the night before and she had opened up the gun and shown him that it was loaded.

When I got home I went into the garage and discovered that the tin where I had hidden the bullets was empty. She must have seen me going into the garage with them. Supin was like the Bluffer, she never missed anything.

The next day George and I confronted Supin. George was already beginning to waver over the robbery and we both knew that this was a situation that could not continue.

But to my surprise Supin handed over the gun and the ammunition without a word. By that time she'd had enough of it.

George hid the gun under the bed in his house and I tucked the bullets away in the loft.

Years later, after the operation and when we were looking back on our lives, I recall her taking my arm and saying softly, ' You done the right thing when you took the gun back. I wasn't myself then.'

But in those days I didn't go down to the casino every night. Sometimes I stayed home and watched the television or read or contemplated trying to write a novel.

If Supin came home late and I was in bed she would give a toot on the horn and I would come down. If her legs were bad that night I would have to carry her in. She would go up piggy back and she used to think that was funny as well.

On another occasion, it was early morning and she had been out all night fishing, she was stopped and reprimanded by a policeman for driving home while eating a piece of toast.

But these were strange times. I have to put my pen down now and close my eyes and check I am not dreaming this one.

My recollection is clear. It is six o clock in the morning. I wake up. The bedroom door is opening and two policemen are helping Supin in. They have found her asleep in the car.

Normally policemen would take this seriously. But as usual she has charmed them and they are all smiles. I can see her hand reaching to her pocket and I think for a moment she is going to take out a coin and tip them.

But the night Mr Chong first appeared in our house she must have crept in very softly because I didn't hear anything at all.

With everything else that was going on at the time why did I take such offence when I went into the spare room in the morning to find Mr Chong fast asleep in the bed? With his great age and his snowy white hair I don't suppose he was planning to jump on my wife's, or anyone else's, bones.

But that day for some reason the worm did turn.

I shouted, 'For God's sake George is enough. I won't have us taking in people we don't know. There are children in the house. We can't carry on like this. He has to go.' But Supin was like the Bluffer. She never took a step back even when she was wrong. She was feet forward, fists up and scrap as dirty as needs be. That was part of her strategy.

I can only suppose that Mr Chong had nowhere else to stay that night. We never asked him where he got the gun he gave to Ivor though Jackie said he still retained 'connections' with Hong Kong.

I have so many memories of that time that if I wrote for the next five years I could never get them all down.

It's late afternoon, sun glinting on the water. Supin is fishing at Mutton Cove. I arrive in the Mondeo to pick her up. Just as we are starting to wrap things up she yells, 'It's so lovely here, I'm going for a swim,' and takes a step off the pier. Luckily I grab her in time and bundle her into the car.

The following week we went in to see John Gibson. 'Ah yes well,' he explained, brow furrowing slightly, 'Bromocriptine can cause hallucinations.'

There are times that this strange film of all our lives is capable of spooling back and forward of its own accord.

Now, quite clearly, I have a memory of being at the Bluffers. It is the time after they have left Wales and moved to the Irish Republic.

The Bluffer and my mother have bought Ballyarr yet another mansion with holes in the roof and leaking pipes.

The Bluffer has invited Norbert for lunch. Norbert is Austrian and was at one time a secretary to a Nobel prize winner. He arrives in an old VW Polo with a slow puncture in a front tyre. He explains that he cannot afford to repair it just at the moment due to a shortage of funds. He and the Bluffer are soon in deep discussion on some business that involves transporting certain goods across the border from the North via The Londonderry & Lough Swilly Bus Company. Norbert is also in serious dispute with his wife Helga who escaped from the fire bombing in Dresden as a child and walked to Hamburg. They share a house and a dozen cats and some dogs. Norbert is consulting the Bluffer as to what is to be done re his domestic situation. We are there en famille and Supin is to cook the lunch.

My job is to look after the children but I still have time to watch Supin as she works in the kitchen. It is the same as the casino. She is absorbed in what she is doing and so is moving freely.

That lunch time she produced a feast which, if I recall correctly, included spare ribs coated in honey, spicy fish cakes and dishes of pork in ginger and prawns in chilli. When we have finished Norbert, who is a great gourmand and who has lived all over the world, declares it the best meal he has ever eaten.

The point of this story is to illustrate that Supin, in her original and brilliant way, is starting to express herself by means other than by speech.

She has always had her own peculiar interpretation of the English language. Some of her inventions are so odd even I find them difficult to grasp. But at other moments she is spot on. She says people sometimes find it hard to understand her because, ' I a bit rumbly now,' which is an original and accurate description.

This difficulty with speech is heightened because Parkinson's disease has started to attack her vocal chords, lowering the pitch of her voice and blurring her delivery.

As a result a vicious circle is beginning to develop. After so many times of being asked to repeat herself she is just about ready to give up. She feels that people are not making the effort to understand her.

In the end I become the public face for both of us. I do the talking and interpreting, while she gets on with her cooking, gardening, fishing, gambling, even carpentry. And in the later days there is the memoir and the temple.

It was about that time that Supin also took a step that every woman should take. She began to dress and look exactly the way she wanted. She stopped caring what anyone else thought.

I took a series of photographs of her fishing down at Mutton Cove and brought them into a studio on Duke Street in Devonport to get them printed up and enlarged. I had given up printing my own pictures when we left Ireland. When I turned up at the studio to pick them up the girl on the counter said, ' Oh yes, you've come for those pictures of that lovely Korean man.'

From the point where Supin used to fish at Mutton Cove it is possible to see the Breakwater in the middle of the Sound. Supin said that was where she wanted her ashes scattered when she died. And that is what we did when the time came.

Tony, one of the Mutton Cove fisherman, took us out in his boat. He cut the engine by the Breakwater. We threw bunches of roses over the side along with the ashes but as we had forgotten to prepare speeches we just watched her drift slowly away.

When I am in town now I go up on to the Hoe and look out over to the Breakwater and know that she is there. Sometimes I sit for a long time thinking how things might have been and wishing I could have made it all better.

## 19

Across the front of this ancient red file the Bluffer has used a black felt tip pen to write the word Counterpart. After that he has roughly underlined it.

The file may be old enough to have begun its life during the Bluffer's army days, but it is more likely, in my view, that it came from the factory in Wales.

I have been trying to find another way into the Bluffer's mind so I have been going through pictures of him and have arranged a selection.

In the earliest picture I can find, he is between his mother and father, Chris and Harald, walking along a sea front. I wonder where that is. I don't think it is Beer. They could be on the pier at Weston super Mare but it is difficult to tell. He looks about fourteen. His face is wide open. I am sure even then he is asking questions and offering opinions.

Then there are other pictures. With my mother, with Alison, with me, on holiday, in Wales, in Ireland. The hair is going slowly grey, then white, but the look is always there. Assured, open, smiling, confident.

It is the war photos that are different. Here he is serious, grave almost. He is certainly aware of his responsibilities.

So what is it all about Dad? What made you decide to embark on this mad adventure? Did you think you were strong enough to hold the entire world above your head? Were you planning to save us all?

One possibility is that a vessel with so much superstructure needs a good lot of balance down below otherwise she will turn turtle.

Does that analogy also hold to a giant ice berg carrying most of its bulk below the surface?

No.

The manuscript is actually the counterpart to this book.

What is not included here, should be there. The two halves should slot together.

It is like one of those optical puzzles. To begin with it looks like a bird but blink and look again the other way and it is a rabbit.

It is an experiment, there are flaws, I can see where he has got tired and his mind has wandered.

It is also a work doomed to fail, he has set himself an impossible task, but it is a heroic effort.

The more I read it, the more I admire it. Not because of its quality, it is disgusting, pornographic, depraved, certainly in parts quite mad, and certainly unpublishable, but because of its intent.

So what did you say to yourself old man? That I am only following nature's pattern? That for all the light that is emitted into the world there is also an equivalent amount of darkness?

Or were you being even more ambitious than that. Were you searching for the plan that lay behind it all?

As a countryman The Bluffer understood the symmetry of nature. He would have been aware how delicately it was all balanced.

That first time I managed to read the opening twenty pages before I had to stop and go into the bathroom and vomit into the toilet bowl.

The book contains sexual details so pornographic and disgusting that they turn the stomach. Every type of sexual deviation, every type of abuse, every type of torture is detailed. There are images of death and hunger and rape and murder. The manuscript is soaked in blood. There are detailed descriptions of conditions in the concentration camps and a calculation of how many lashes a prisoner could withstand before he died. I put my nose to the page. The whole thing stinks of shit and blood. There are pages of sickening personal, sexual and racial abuse. If it had fallen into the wrong hands it could have been used as a manifesto. If Hitler himself had read it he would have nodded sagely. In this bizarre history, which lasts for hundreds of pages, every massacre, every murder, every fraud, every terrible execution, every act of unkindness, is listed.

There are chapters on the massacres in Rwanda with discussion on the type of killing knife used. Then from photos he has found on the internet he has made an estimate of the maximum permitted weight of a rock in a Muslim stoning. He has written a note in the margin, as usual in pencil asking, 'Is this like being hit by a cricket ball?'

He is everywhere, from large events to small, going back and forth. He is searching for detail of anti Semitism in Ireland and has been reading about the Limerick Pogrom. He has added in pencil a note, 'Fucking Catholic Church! Typical!'

There are pages where he has got muddled. The intensity of it all must have disturbed him. In a long study of the type of music played over the loud speakers at concentration camps, and a detailed entry on the music of Schubert, there are also extensive notes on the state of his garden.

One reads: 'No fruit on trees. Very poor crop. Bees not pollinating. Not good this year.'

Then he records the detail of a bad meal he has eaten in a local restaurant. There is a draft of a letter to the Environmental Health Officer at the local council in which he says that the establishment should be shut down, but the letter appears never to have been sent.

He has also recorded price and quality of vegetables in shops and declared himself 'pleasantly surprised' at the results.

But then he is back on track and writing about Germany after the war. He was there so the experience is first hand.

I close my eyes and imagine the scene. All I can see are ruins and buildings blown apart. Skies are always grey and dark and it is permanently cold. Everyone is hungry.

There are details of Russian prisoners he interrogated. I look out of the window. There is no reason why some of them should not have come to Ireland.

According to the phone book there is a Mr K in Derry and a Mr V in Belfast. But there is no point in ringing. The odds are too long.

But it is certainly possible that an elderly gentleman, I can almost see his face, is at this moment looking out of his window, as I am doing now, watching the first blossom on the trees. And is he recalling as he does so, that tall serious Englishman who held his life in the palm of his hand all those years ago? It is strange that whoever he is, wherever he is, he knew the Bluffer before I did.

In one passage of the book Ravensbruck concentration camp is mentioned several times. I get the feeling that the Bluffer has been there. Then he is excited. He has been listening to Schubert. 'That is it!' He has noted. 'That is exactly what it was like!'

There is nothing in his pile of CDs but a search on line finds the music and soon a Schubert quintet is coming out of the speakers and filling the house.

The bleak sadness of the music seeps into everything. When I close my eyes I get a sudden image, almost cartoonlike, of a young woman. She is in striped concentration camp pyjamas and she is hanging onto the wire of the camp perimeter. She is stick thin and desperate. She stares plaintively out into the distance. Then the music changes. There is a shaft of light and the Bluffer is on his knees cutting a hole in the wire. She is crawling out through the hole! Then they are running across the frozen ground into the forest, dashing and jerking along in the manner of black and white silent movie stars. Then the music changes again and now they are in a cafe in Vienna dancing brilliantly under bright electric lights!

That afternoon I learn that Dietrich Fischer-Dieskau, with whom the Bluffer shared the page for his Daily Telegraph obituary, was known for his performance of Schubert's Winterreise song cycle. So is that somehow more than a co incidence?

There is also the folio of German etchings I found as I was clearing out his things. Do they fit into this strange pattern as well?

Thinking to give an illustration of what he was doing I copied out several passages intending to add them into this narrative.

But I stop when I realise that if those passages are included here they will have to come out of Counterpart and I will have ruined the symmetry of his project.

There is also something else that is odd about Counterpart. The more I read it the longer it becomes. And every time I turn a page I can feel that the book is becoming heavier.

I take a break for lunch and to do other things and then return to it in the early evening.

He is burrowing back into the past. Germany and the wars have long been left behind. The cruelties of the Middle Ages are being described now. It has grown dark by the time I look up again. I get up and stretch. I am getting bored. He is beginning to lose the thread. He is mixing things up again.

He has begun to design a new type of road junction which he says will reduce traffic accidents and wants to get it patented. I have to force myself to continue.

Then suddenly he has found his focus again. I turn the pages and we are rattling down dark alleys and passage ways until finally we are coming to rooms which are locked and barred and to which even he has no access. After that, exhausted, I give up.

He has created a mad, dark, anarchic library, with no beginning, middle or end. I close the file. It is like rummaging through someone's dustbin.

In the end I was too tired to even want a drink. I went upstairs to the bedroom undressed got into bed and in a moment had entered a long dreamless sleep.

## 20

It took me a month to walk from Genoa to Ravenna. I could have done it more quickly, but I was not in a hurry. I made the long climb up to the top of the Passo del Bocco. After that I fell in love with the valley of the River Taro. If I could have found a secluded cabin in the woods on one of those hillsides, I would surely have given up my long hike and settled down there. But I didn't, instead tramping along the Po Valley, dog legging it via Parma, Reggio, Modena and finally Bologna. The only exciting thing that happened to me on that gloomy plain was getting caught, early one morning, with the mist still down, on the Reggio by pass. The cars whizzed past my nose and I was only saved by a bus driver who stopped and took me into Reggio. Then finally I arrived at Ravenna and the Adriatic. After that I made a short diversion by train to visit Venice before considering my next move.

I had earlier missed a section of Portugal due to the difficulty of walking on narrow roads and now I took my second short cut. The Bluffer and Supin were becoming impatient with me so I decided to cross the Adriatic and begin once more in Dubrovnik in Croatia.

In Dubrovnik the cruise ships were all lined up in the port and I thought of how aptly Vilis had described them as the Pig Boats. I had seen them entering the lagoon in Venice, their superstructures taller than the ancient buildings they were passing. They had looked grotesque and alien.

But when I walked out of Dubrovnik and crossed the border from Croatia into Republika Srpska in Bosnia and Herzegovina I fell in love with the Balkans.

The Pig Boaters and the glitzy coast suddenly belonged to another world. At the first village I came to, which was really just a collection of rough looking houses, I stopped at a shop and bought a tin of hot dogs and a bottle of beer and a loaf of bread. The shelves were poorly stocked and the people shabbily dressed. Neither were they particularly friendly but I didn't care.

I camped out that first night in a half built house. During the night a convoy of cars passed at high speed.

The house stood alone and I thought no one had seen me but the bush telegraph must have been working because early in the morning the owner arrived. I heard his car draw up and a door slam as he got out. But when he realised I was a foreigner he lost interest and left me alone.

As I set off a little while later I noted the signs warning people not to leave the road due to the danger of unexploded mines. (These were left over from the latest Balkan war). Then I came across dozens of abandoned houses. Their roofs had been burned and they stood empty and open to the weather. I could see that the scrub vegetation was beginning to reclaim this land, creeping over fences and walls and into the abandoned houses.

When I crossed into Montenegro the devastation of war faded behind me. The villages seemed to be well tended and the citizens, on the whole, in better humour than those in Republica Srpska.

However I felt uneasy when I entered the town of Nicsic. The steelworks that used to employ thousands had, so I was told, fallen on hard times and workers had been laid off. The town also seemed to be curiously silent with most people on foot. In the parks the grass was knee high as if someone were waiting to cut it for hay.

The other thing I noted, and it seems to be true of many Balkan towns I passed through, was the disproportionate number of betting shops, coffee shops and body building studios.

Then in the hotel in Nicsic a Bulgarian man sold me an old Soviet military map of the region and this showed a path going due East across the mountains toward the town of Kolasin. The weather forecast I had seen on the TV in the hotel restaurant that morning was good so I decided to follow the path. By avoiding the route south to Podgorica I could cut almost a week off my journey.

So I set off on a two day walk toward the village of Morakovo which was at the foot of the mountain. The first night I put up my tent at the edge of a small village and was soon surrounded by a group of school children to whom I handed out chocolate. The next day, when I arrived at Morakovo, which again is only a collection of wooden farm houses, I was invited to eat lunch and drink home made Rakia with a family after I had asked them directions.

Here it should be stated that in this part of the Balkans, as in Gulliver's Travels, the traveller from a far off land feels that he has come across a race of giants.

The family with whom I ate lunch were all over six foot tall and the walls of their house were decorated with pictures of the basketball teams for which they played. In cafes and bars I had already noted that the chairs were larger than they would have been at home.

It was mid afternoon when I left the family and turned off the road and using my old Soviet map set off up the path.

As I walked steadily uphill I thought about sticking to footpaths for the rest of my journey. On the footpaths there are no cars, no noise, no people. Then I stopped to look down over the valley. Directly below me I could see the house, now tiny as a doll's house, where I had eaten lunch. In the distance was the outline of the town of Nicsic. The only sound I could hear was the wind in the trees. That night I pitched my tent by the side of the path and cooked up my dinner on my little camping stove. After that I stood drinking a bottle of beer looking out on to the valley as the darkness descended.

But the following morning after I had set off again I had a nasty surprise when turning a corner I found the path blocked by a heavy wall of snow.

For a few moments I stood there. I hadn't expected snow at all. Then I put down my pack and spent an hour trying to find a way around the snow. But when it was obvious that it stretched a long way back I reluctantly had to turn around and go back down.

I had already found that my Soviet map, though detailed in many respects, it gave both width and depth of rivers, was in other ways alarmingly inaccurate. So I had no confidence that it would guide me over the snow covered mountain to the town of Kolasin on the other side.

Coming down I was gripped by a horrible head ache and stopped to drink at a stream and rest on the grass and close my eyes for a moment to let it pass.

The family in the village were surprised that the pass was blocked so early in the season. The truth was, I suppose, that nobody else went up there except the odd shepherd.

In the end the afternoon bus which stopped in the village took me back into Nicsic.

After that I caught another bus to Podgorica where I stayed at a backpackers refuge run by an American called Brad.

His girl friend, who was twenty years his junior, only came out of her room to eat and pee. Brad told me over a late night bottle of vodka that she was running an internet counselling service for people who were suicidal.

After that I took the bus to Kolasin where I could see the crest of snow on the mountain on the other side of the river. For the sake of a couple of miles I had done a diversion of almost a hundred. That night I wished I had carried on. But the Soviet map was not accurate and though I was well equipped as a routard I was in no way a mountaineer.

I stayed several days in Kolasin renting a wooden chalet from a family. It was pleasant enough, later in the season people would come to ski, but after a few days I was eager to move on.

The family had tied up a dog in a kennel in the garden and I fed it morning and night, boiling up rice and hot dogs. I never saw the family feed the dog so when I set off again I left a note on the kitchen counter saying they should take better care of their dog.

## 21

The Bluffer and my mother ran the hotel in Wales for several years before selling up and moving to the Irish Republic. There they bought another derelict property that was far too big for them. It had the usual leaking roof and dry rot.

I said to the Bluffer that he had to get out of Wales in his socks because he was being chased by the tax man but he denied this angrily.

The house was called Ballyarr and it was in County Donegal. A Wikipedia search shows that it was built in 1780 and that by 1850 it was in the hands of a landlord called George Hill who at the time owned twenty three thousand acres in Donegal and had a reputation for summarily evicting his tenants.

Then I note, with some pride, a reference on another internet site to Ballyarr House:

'It was bought in 1974 by Ian Smith, a former hotelier and British war hero, and his artist wife Peggy.'

Later, when the Bluffer and my mother had moved on again, it was bought by a couple from London who were involved in television and newspapers. The Bluffer went back once and told me afterwards he had been shocked by what they had done to it. I remember him shaking his head and saying sadly, 'You know they've done up the house so it looks like a tart's parlour.'

The Bluffer and my mother arrived during the height of the troubles. The border and the city of Derry, a real hot spot where Martin McGuinness and the rest of the IRA gang were operating, was only half an hour away. By rights he should have been run out of town. He was the caricature of an Englishman, down to the moustache, the accent, the war record and the political views. But the Bluffer was fully aware of the position. He was shrewd. After all he was the author of Counterpart. He had it all worked out. He knew he had to keep his head down and get the lie of the land and build a power base before he could successfully operate.

So he formed the necessary strategic alliances. He was quickly on good terms with the inspector of taxes and with senior customs officers. He also had his foot soldiers on the ground. He had his mechanics and his repair men, his gardeners and his builders. He had all the experts in all the necessary fields. He could have gone to war with the troops he had assembled. He even had the clergy speaking up for him. (Years later three of them spoke at his funeral and there was not a dry eye in the house when they had finished).

But was it at this moment in his life that he made a miscalculation? Did he fully understand the Irish? Should he have known that when the pendulum of the Irish character swings, it swings with a real ferocity?

But that was for the future.

This was a period in their lives when both my mother and the Bluffer flowered. My mother became absorbed in her painting and it did not take the Bluffer long to realise that in this part of Ireland he had fallen among people who had the same outlook on life as he did - that rules were there to be surmounted and that payment of tax was a last and desperate option. The Bluffer was in his element. When I look at of photographs of him then, he is sleek as a silver fox. He is planning, calculating, computing. The days of penury are over. Thanks to the hotel and the brandy smuggling they once again have capital. The fiasco of the failed clothing business is a book closed long ago.

For the first two years when they were in the Irish Republic the Bluffer and my mother were in seventh heaven. They renovated Ballyarr and made it comfortable. They had a good circle of friends in the Anglo Irish hierarchy. There were drinks parties and invitations to dinner. My mother was even invited to open the village fete.

This is the time when she began to paint and soon she was being invited to exhibit her work in local galleries. Alison and her family were also only an hour away across the border in Northern Ireland. (When my mother became ill they sold Ballyarr and moved to Northern Ireland to be near Alison, but that was still some years away).

The Bluffer was advising a small engineering business while at the same time working on a plan to install a turbine on the river which ran through his property. In the evenings he continued with Counterpart. He was also using the border to his advantage. In those days there were customs controls between the Republic and Northern Ireland. There were also sharp price differentials which meant there was a lively smuggling trade.

Then one evening, a perfect summer's evening. Everything calm, not a sound. The swallows are flying high. He has been mowing the grass in the field in front of the house. Flying along on his old Fordson tractor with a gang mower behind. Then he has stopped at the far end of the field and has turned to look back at the house. He can see a faint movement in the kitchen, which is my mother getting supper. She has seen him stop too and is wondering what he is thinking. He looks around at everything he has got and everything he has achieved - and then he realises suddenly that he is bored. He realises that his life lacks excitement. Over the next few days he considers long and hard. My mother notices the change, but she leaves him alone. She hopes they are not going to sell up and move on again.

In the end he resolves the problem by renewing an old friendship with Ambrose McGonigal, now a High Court judge in Belfast. At the same time he develops a new friendship with Edward Pineles, a London property developer. My mother wholeheartedly approves of Ambrose McGonigal but is decidedly unsure, to begin with, of Edward Pineles.

Ambrose was godfather to my sister Alison. He had fought in the same irregular unit as the Bluffer in the war. They had shared many adventures together. They had both been awarded the Military Cross, though later in the war The Bluffer was awarded a Bar to his MC, which was a very rare honour. Mac, as he was known, was a great drinker, and a great fighter - on and off the battlefield. The Bluffer said that once he had a couple of pints inside him he would take on anyone he met, friend or foe, with both fists. The Bluffer said many was the time he had to take him to hospital to have his cuts and bruises tended. But the years have changed him. He made his name as a barrister at the enquiry into the sinking of the Princess Victoria. This was the car ferry that went down in the Irish Sea in 1953 with the loss of a hundred and thirty three lives. Now he sits grimly on the bench in the High Court in Belfast doling out long sentences to young men with much the same attitude to life as he had thirty years before.

Because of the situation in Northern Ireland at that time Mac had to be very careful over his security. He certainly could not risk travelling across the border to the south. The IRA had excellent intelligence capabilities and he would have been in grave danger. So instead the Bluffer used to go up to Belfast and they would have dinner together and talk about old times.

It was only when I was going through the Bluffer's papers that I realised the extent of his meetings with Mac. My mother had assumed that they had been discussing the old days. On occasion she was invited along as well and they had a pleasant evening, en famille, with Mac and his wife.

But looking through the papers I can see from notes of meetings that there had been other ideas. Mac was in a difficult position. He saw and heard everything. He sat in his court all day, confronted by the most dangerous and violent men in the province. He listened to their pleas and their justifications. He knew everything that both sides got up to, the army and the IRA.

Then I discovered that the pair of them had jointly begun to sketch out a series of articles. The Bluffer was going to submit them to the Irish Times under the pen name Points North.

He has kept carbons of most of them in the filing cabinet with his papers. I spread them out on the desk as I eat my lunch.

The Bluffer's original mind and Mac's fine legal brain should have produced some scintillating stuff.

I thought of the files full of original ideas that I had gone through where the Bluffer had let his mind run free.

Yesterday I had read of his idea, there were diagrams and calculations included, to dam another local river. He had worked out that the fall of the water, if channelled properly via a turbine, would provide electricity for the whole village almost free of charge.

In the drafts for the Points North articles the usual subjects of the day were discussed - cross border co operation, political status for prisoners, the suitability of the army in a close quarters urban war.

But with the possibility of publication it seems that their minds have frozen. It is very dry stuff and lacks imagination. I had hoped for something that showed original thinking, but this is all very wooden.

I look out of the window and sip my coffee.

Perhaps it is Mac's influence. The Bluffer had let slip to my mother that, since his elevation to the bench he had become 'quite rigid' in his views.

This suspicion was confirmed when in a draft of an article which was critical of the performance of the army some parts had been crossed out. Then there was a note in a hand that was not the Bluffer's, so I presume it must have been Mac's, saying, 'I don't think so!'

It should also be remembered that both Mac and the Bluffer for all their courage and their dare devil exploits are at heart very conservative men. Perhaps they baulked at taking on the establishment so frontally.

But then as I am about to close the folder and replace it in the filing cabinet I turn the page and see another note, which is definitely not for publication which makes me sit up straight in my chair.

The fuzziness of the proposed newspaper articles is suddenly gone. Everything has come sharply into focus.

It is all organised. Notes typed up properly. Twelve invited for a dinner. The Bluffer makes thirteen. Only thing not given, deliberately, is a location.

The Bluffer has even drawn up a table plan. After all these years I still recognise the names. They are the elite, the most influential men in the province. There are also representatives from the mainland. Mac is at the head of the table and the Bluffer, as his adjutant, is to his side.

At dinner the conversation seems to have been general but after the meal the serious discussion begins. I am trying to grab the undercurrent. The Bluffer has typed clearly in his notes: 'The atmosphere is electric.'

Then a certain X, he is still alive so I am not going to name him, or even give any indication of what post he held, except to say that he was a household name, is announcing that he thinks the time is ripe to declare independence.

He is saying that London is tired of the province and its intractable problems and that if the declaration is done quickly and bloodshed is limited it will not stand in its way. Then a senior military figure is on his feet saying that the addresses of all the top IRA leaders, even the ones they think are secret, are all well known. Another politician adds that if the top echelons of the

IRA are taken out quickly, the rest of the Catholic population will come quietly.

The discussion continues for several hours. A lot of detail is discussed. There is a fear that the government in the south will be hostile. There is also concern about further civil unrest if internment is re introduced. The economy is described as fragile and there is worry over the reaction of the Americans. The Bluffer has added afterwards in his trade mark pencil note in the margin, 'Talk about smoke filled rooms!'

Finally a vote is taken and it is eight to four in favour of declaring independence.

At the conclusion of the meeting, under the typewritten notes, the Bluffer has written, again by hand, 'A momentous decision.'

When the last of the guests are gone I imagine Mac and the Bluffer pushing back their chairs and sharing a final brandy.

How you would have enjoyed that evening old man! You would have been in your element. Up to your ears in it. Right up your street, along with the war exploits and the brandy smuggling and Counterpart.

Nothing came of it of course. In those days in Northern Ireland events moved quickly. Some new crisis probably over took them. But thirty years later it is still an incendiary document. I read through the list of names again. You always manage it old man. You are always just there, backing quietly into the limelight.

As to Ambrose it is for his family to write the story of his life as he is also now dead.

Edward Pineles, was very different from Ambrose McGonigal. He was a London property developer who always sailed close to the wind.

They had met at the show jumping at Hickstead. It was Peter, the Bluffer's brother, who worked for the tobacco company W.D. and H.O. Wills in Bristol, at the time sponsoring Hickstead, who made the introductions. My mother loved going to Hickstead which at the time was run by a man called Douglas Bunn, another colourful character.

Edward was a dark heavy man with a beard. The Bluffer said that the family background was central European and that there was, ' Certainly Jewish blood there as well.'

Edward had served in the Navy during the war and had been in charge of a gun turret on a battleship. After the war he had gone into property in London where he had made his fortune. However at some point he had come under suspicion of bribing a planning officer and it was anticipated that the police were going to make an arrest. Journalists were also beginning to write critical articles. So along with George, his private detective, who later married his daughter Laura, he decamped to France buying a mansion called Les Valettes in the hills behind Nice.

The Bluffer loved going to Les Valettes and he often took my mother. He said Edward was highly intelligent and very well read and that he was interested in prison reform. Other people said he was a bully and vindictive and treated his family badly. In the afternoons the Bluffer and my mother would play tennis with Douglas the Goanese butler and then Edward would take them both to dinner in Nice.

Strangely enough in my walk across Europe I went by that house but it was locked up and empty by then.

Edward and the Bluffer had great adventures together. It was Edward who showed the Bluffer how to operate a Swiss bank account and for a while, or so it seemed to me, the Bluffer fell under Edward's spell and became his bag man.

But these were strange times in Ireland. As well as revolutionary and criminal turbulence there was money pouring in from Europe. Fortunes were also being made with cross border smuggling. It seemed at times that the country was awash with cash. Government ministers, including the Prime Minister Charles Haughey, were all on the take. The Bluffer was in a small way able to benefit from this. He was now, thanks to Edward, an expert on getting money out of the country and into 'safe havens' and could offer discreet advice. On occasion he even did the run himself.

Then Edward, the former patriot, who has a very good portrait of the Queen on his wall, and who drinks whiskey but who won't have wine at the table, buys a share of a Republican magazine in Dublin as an act of vengeance on the country which he considers has spurned him. The Bluffer goes on the board to protect his interests. But here the Bluffer makes a mistake. He is out of his depth. When he tries to bring some sort of order to the finances the gimlet eyed hard men of the Republican movement just stare at him without blinking.

Without the Bluffer realising it, the wheels are beginning to turn. For the first time in his life he is making enemies and very soon they are going to come back and take their vengeance.

## 22

Two months after Supin and George announced their intention to rob the casino everything fell apart.

I had been out, it was a Wednesday. A group of us always met up on a Wednesday night. I took a taxi home and as I walked up the path to the house I noted a strange car in the driveway. There was also a light on in the front room.

When I got inside I saw that it was Ivor and that he was sitting next to Supin on the sofa. On the table in front of them was Supin's jewellery collection and he appeared to be selecting the best pieces. I could see she was close to tears.

For most women their jewellery collection has a sentimental attraction and is extremely precious to them. But for Supin rings and bracelets (with the honourable exception of her wedding ring, which only disappeared once into the pawn shop and was recovered a short while later) were a form of currency that came and went. I recall once that we went into a jewellery shop on New George Street and got a valuation on two rings that raised an eyebrow from the jeweller. For a moment we were rich, but a couple of days later they were gone.

But still there are limits. And certainly when a man comes home to find a particularly nasty individual who is known to be a money lender pawing over his wife's jewellery collection it causes a reaction.

There were other things that had been boiling up as well. Because we were short of money I had to keep a tight control on our budget. This was an inevitable source of friction. I still loved Supin but at the same time I was exasperated by her activities in the casino. She was also frustrated with me. The previous evening she had told me, in a very direct way, that my reluctance to act as getaway driver was now threatening the whole robbery plan. Additionally on those Wednesday nights I certainly drank more than was good for me.

So at that moment, with all these pressures, something snapped and I ran across the room and grabbed hold of Ivor by his shoulders and struck him several sharp blows to the side of the head.

Then while he was still stunned, and before I had time to think of what I was doing, I caught hold of him by the neck, ran him down the path in a sort of headlock, opened the door to his car and threw him inside. As he drove off I smacked my hand against a side window and yelled out, 'I'll kill you, you bastard, if you ever set foot in this house again.'

As I walked back up to the house I stopped and looked around. I was astonished by what I had done.

My action must have registered with Supin because she trod round me warily after that. For several weeks she stayed at home and cooked, gardened and mended. There was no mention of the robbery and no requests for funds to go gambling. It occurred to me then that if I had taken a firmer stance at the beginning our lives would have been much better.

I saw Ivor in the casino but he kept his distance. My last word to all of them on the robbery was that if they continued with their planning they would soon cross a line where they could be charged with conspiracy.

But then we received the news that altered all our plans.

We were sitting at the table. As usual, in those difficult days, our evening meal had been eaten with a minimum of conversation. Then Supin cleared her throat and said sharply, 'You heard what happened or what?'

I knew by the tone of the voice that it was something important and I guessed that it was to do with the robbery plan.

Finally she came out with it.

'They found Ivor up on the Moor. Someone cut off his head with a chainsaw.'

For a moment I looked at her. Then I stared down at the plate and then at the wall and around the room and then back at her again.

If I didn't hear Supin clearly, her speech could at times be difficult to understand, I had to ask her to repeat herself. This always annoyed her. She would reply that I must have something wrong with my hearing and that I needed to wash out my ears.

But on this occasion I heard correctly the first time.

We sit for a long while after that.

Ivor Dryer, money lender and would be leader of our bank robbing gang, has been found dead, minus his head, at a place called Clearbrook on the edge of Dartmoor.

Steven Williams, according to the television news, has been charged with the murder. He is one of the doormen at the casino. He is a man we know well and like. He is always friendly to us. He even goes fishing with George and Supin.

The following day we set George to work and soon he had the full story.

On the day of the killing, according to George's researches, Ivor went to see Steven Williams at his house. Steven Williams owed Ivor a thousand pounds and Ivor wanted his money back. Ivor also suspected that Steven Williams was sleeping with his ex wife. The confrontation between the two men then turned into a violent fight and Steven Williams finally stabbed Ivor several times in the back with a kitchen knife.

Six months later the case came before Exeter Crown Court and lasted two days. Steven Williams entered a plea of not guilty to murder, saying he acted in self defence. Supin wanted to go, but I told her to stay away. Instead I sent George and he sat through both days of the hearing.

The details were gruesome. I thought of the Bluffer and his book Counterpart. It would have probably been too small an incident for him to record but he would certainly have understood what it was all about.

George told us that instead of disposing of Ivor's body straight away Steven Williams kept it under the bed in his flat for four days.

During that period he went to work as normal on the door at the casino. In the daytime he also followed his normal routine, even going for a dental check up.

George told us how Steven Williams bought an axe and a chainsaw and then drove the body up to Clearbrook and set about his grizzly task. A point that came out in court, that we had not known before, was that in addition to decapitating Ivor, Steven Williams also removed both his arms and legs.

After that Steven Williams made a clumsy attempt to burn the body parts before finally wrapping the remains up in plastic sheeting and dumping them in a shallow ditch. But carelessly he left a sticker with his address on the plastic sheeting and so he was traced immediately by the police.

I asked George to study Steven Williams as he sat in the dock during the trial. He reported back that his face was impassive.

What was going through his mind as all this is happening? Was he numb with shock, going on autopilot, blocking out the horror? Or was he full of embarrassment and shame and remorse?

Personally I was relieved that with Ivor gone the robbery plan fell.

Steven Williams was convicted by the jury of murder and sentenced to life imprisonment with a minimum term of sixteen years. All this is true.

## 23

Over the next few days, at the Bluffer's house in Northern Ireland, I read several hundred more pages of Counterpart. As I did so I noted that, in an inverse of the normal, the more I read the further away the end became.

It was also obvious, as I turned the pages, that the manuscript was steadily increasing in weight. By the end of the second day the office desk was beginning to creak and I had to transfer to a sturdier table in the living room.

Even though the Bluffer is describing the worst excesses of which humans are capable he is writing with an eloquence and fluency that draws me on.

Did he think that if he could wrap up just the smallest portion of the world's unhappiness and misery, a churchman would probably have used the word evil, that he could somehow save the rest of us from having to experience it?

I don't know if that was his intent. And of course, not having his overview, I have no idea if he has had any success. It could also be that he wrote Counterpart just to show that the world was made up of equal parts of light and shadow.

As far as I know I am the only person who has read this document. I have not discussed it with anyone else for fear they would think it too disgusting and probably mad.

But they didn't know the Bluffer the way I did. They didn't know his capacity for original thought. They didn't know, for instance, that he had employed a private detective to track down the man I might have become if I had reached Veracruz.

The Bluffer was also capable of taking on challenges that the rest of us would never consider. The only difference was that this project he kept private.

In my opinion its genesis was in Germany after the war.

While he was happy to gas on all night about his other war time adventures he was always a little more ' piano' when it came to Germany. Strangely there are also no pictures of him at all from that period.

In fact the clues are very thin on the ground. They come down to no more than his discovery of Schubert, his pride at not sending any of the Russian prisoners he interrogated home and several mentions of Ravensbruck concentration camp.

Was there a woman?

As he got older, and generally over a glass of whiskey, he would hint at certain exotic liaisons, but I always thought he was inventing most of them.

He adored my mother and they had a relationship which would be the envy of many people today.

But there are certain clues.

There are hundreds of family pictures. I spread them out on the floor and then compared them to the pictures I had found in the file of the man and the woman on the cruise liner.

It took me several hours but in the end I discovered a pattern. It has the elements of a detective story but the clue really was a cigarette holder.

The oldest picture is a black and white snap of the Bluffer in a pub. He is with a group of his rugby team mates and next to him is an attractive young woman. It is possible to see that in her right hand, which is down by her side, she has a cigarette in a holder.

Then there is another black and white picture of a blonde woman standing by a suitcase at Temple Meads station in Bristol. She is raising a cigarette, again in a holder, to her lips.

The last one, at least twenty years later on, is a Polaroid. The quality of the colour is poor. It is taken in the dining room of our hotel at Llugwy where she is among a group of six. The hair is differently styled but again there is the cigarette holder.

The next task is to compare these three photos with the face of the woman on the cruise liner. This is difficult because the pictures are all taken at different times up to forty years apart. The quality of the photocopies is also poor.

The woman on the cruise liner does not have the tell tale cigarette holder but it has to be the same person.

Then in the background to the pictures on the cruise liner I note the skyline of a city.

A check on Google, what did we do without Uncle Google and his friend Mr Wikipedia, brings up the skylines of half a dozen European ports. Half an hour's study then brings up a good match to the skyline of Bremerhaven.

But that is it. Nothing more. Perhaps in the end it was something entirely different that persuaded the Bluffer to start on this fantastic project. If I had been able to ask him I know exactly how he would have answered.

Instead of the normal jovial response he would have said, in a quite different voice, 'Fuck off mate, that has got nothing to do with you,' and shut the drawer of the filing cabinet firmly.

For the next couple of days I listened to a lot of Schubert and the bittersweet notes touched me deeply.

Then in the end, rummaging through a drawer in the bedroom, I came across an old CD and put it on the player.

It comes from ten years ago when we took all our old home cine films and put them together and transferred them first to DVD and then to CD.

I watch as the Bluffer ages, his hair goes from black to grey to silver to white. At times he has put on weight but he appears to be able to lose it again quickly when he wants.

There is Alison on her wedding day, looking beautiful as a film star, flipping back her veil and laughing. There is my mother, my, how good looking you were, on a summers evening on the lawn at Llugwy Hall.

There is a thirty second burst of the interior of Llugwy before we converted it into the hotel. The light is dim, and I have to go over it a couple of times to make sure, but there in what we called the breakfast room and which was later converted into the bar for the hotel sits the same old filing cabinet, the one that contains Counterpart.

The next scene is interesting.

The Bluffer has a table set up by the front door. On the table is a typewriter and next to it is a glass of beer and a plate with a half eaten sandwich.

He is concentrating, typing quickly.

Then my mother, there is no sound to any of these films, must have shouted something to him because he looks up from his typing.

But I watch him in the seconds before he realises my mother is filming him. He is completely different. His typing is quick and urgent. His face is sharp. I play the sequence several times and then sit back shocked. For the first time in my life I have seen a look of fear on the Bluffer's face. He has the face, as he types, of a hunted man. Then he hears my mother's voice and the image dissolves and he gives a cheesy sort of grin.

All these researches he kept from us. We had no idea of the depth of his knowledge. He is able, for instance, to go backward and forwards from the Spanish Inquisition to the French Revolution to Stalin's Gulags with ease.

I take the next day off and ring the local garage and arrange to hire a car.

After Wales the Bluffer and my mother had moved to Ballyarr House in County Donegal in the Irish Republic. But then when my mother got ill their last move was to Northern Ireland to be near my sister Alison and her family.

I trace a route on the map. Cross the border, see Ballyarr. Supin and I used to visit regularly with family. Have a day away and drive around the coast. Get some bracing sea air on the face. Clear the cob webs. Get rid of the stink of that bloody book.

Instead the opposite happened. I stopped in Derry and ended up wiping away those cobwebs in half a dozen crowded pubs rather than on a windswept beach.

I can't recall the names of the pubs or even the streets they were on. It was all random. I told ridiculous stories, bought drinks, made new friends. Then we sang songs till our faces went red with the heat and the drink. I even flirted with a couple of ladies until their husbands appeared.

There was an early evening interlude in a Chinese restaurant where the rice and the pork soaked up the alcohol. As I ate I suddenly realised that Counterpart was now mine and that I had to decide what to do with it.

But that night, after the horror of the detail of the book, I needed the warm touch of humanity. The Bluffer would have enjoyed himself as well. We would have wiped away all the crap, started over again, been the best of pals.

For the following few days the sky was clear and the sun shone and I was able to sit in the garden reading Counterpart. There was a stone mill wheel on a plinth that served as a table. It was sturdy enough to take the manuscript which was becoming very heavy by this time.

Soon we are descending deep into the dark ages. But I am losing my points of reference. He is writing about places and people of which I have never heard. After a couple of afternoons of this I found myself increasingly breaking off to do other tasks.

I had appointments with the solicitor and I had to go to the bank to close up accounts.

In the evenings I listened to Schubert and because I am the Bluffer's son I am sure that a tear came to my eye at exactly the same time as it would have come to his eye.

But then one morning with the weather looking as if it was going to turn and with the manuscript becoming so heavy I feared to turn any more of the pages I'd had enough.

I went into town and filled a can full of petrol and returned to the house. Then I doused the manuscript in the petrol. It had to go, I didn't want that filth around anymore. The Bluffer had made whatever point he was trying to make.

But that was too easy for The Bluffer. He had printed out his book on a special paper that wouldn't burn. In half an hour I had used up all the petrol and the manuscript was still intact. I recalled his war time activities and wondered if he had somehow inversed a procedure. This was the opposite of a one time flimsy or an edible code pad.

After that I went back into the house and telephoned the local council and asked if they had a system for taking away objects that could not be gone into the car.

I was passed through to the waste department but when a girl asked me what it was I needed to get rid of I looked out of the window to the manuscript sitting on the table and said not to worry I would sort it out myself.

Letters from his stockbroker showed that The Bluffer had managed his investments well. There was also a communication from Switzerland which showed that he had a considerable sum on deposit in a bank there.

So, without worrying about the cost, I was able to go into Derry and order an engineering company to make up a secure metal container in which I could transport the manuscript.

When I had got the container home I somehow managed to shovel the manuscript into it. If I had turned any more pages it would certainly have been too heavy. Even the mill wheel table was starting to lurch over by this time. Then I telephoned a specialist removal company to come and take it away.

Three men came the following morning. I had told them the metal container was heavy. But using a small fork lift truck they were able to get the container into the back of the truck.

After that we drove up to Larne and I went down onto the docks and negotiated a price to hire a solid looking fishing boat. Then we parked the truck up against the side of the boat and managed to lever the box on board.

The skipper was unhappy about it. He squinted through the metal slits in the side of the container to satisfy himself that I was not trying to get rid of a body. His boat was also sitting lower in the water than he liked. But finally we set off. The sum that he had received had proved an adequate counter balance to his fears.

When the skipper said we were halfway between Scotland and Ireland the crew manoeuvred the container to the side. When we finally got it into the water the boat righted herself with a great heave as if glad to be rid of such a heavy burden.

Then for a moment the container floated by the side of the boat and we all watched anxiously. The skipper was as keen as I was that it should sink. He knew there was something not right. So a few minutes later when all the air had been forced out and the container had dipped under the waves for the last time we all breathed a sigh of relief. We stayed on watch for a good half hour after that but nothing bobbed back up. After that we returned to Larne.

And that, apart from one strange incident which I will recount later, was the last I heard of Counterpart. I really hope that by its existence it will have done somebody somewhere some good, but personally I was glad to get rid of it.

# 24

The casino buzzed as the gamblers discussed the decapitation on Dartmoor of Ivor Dryer by the doorman Steven Williams. There were some who said he got what he deserved but most people were shocked.

Then the story of how I had attacked Ivor at our house also came out and people asked me about that.

After that Mr Chong's name came up. Somebody had been looking into his background in Hong Kong. Then the whispers started about Supin and her big win.

When George, who was monitoring all this gossip for us, finally reported back that it was now being said that both Supin and Mr Chong had Mafia connections we stopped going to the casino for a bit.

Instead we turned for a moment in the opposite direction, driving up to the Thai Buddhavihara Temple at Kings Bromley in Staffordshire for a break.

The Abbot there is Phra Maha Laow. We have known him for over twenty years, going back to the days when he was a monk at the Buddhapadipa temple in Wimbledon.

Phra Maha Laow greets Supin warmly. But then he greets everyone warmly. Phra Maha Laow is a bundle of energy, never stopping. Like all the monks at the temple his head is shaved and he wears the brown robes. When he walks the robes bustle and billow about him.

There is a memory I have of Phra Maha Laow. After Supin had died and we were looking for a location for our temple in Plymouth I telephoned him because it looked as if we might have found somewhere suitable.

But a week later when he came down to view the property I was shocked to see how ill he looked. So I asked his driver what had happened.

The explanation I got was that he had been released from hospital only a few days previously, there had been an operation for gallstones, and he had strict instructions to rest.

But he had ignored this advice. The previous day he had ordered his driver to take him to Cambridge for a meeting. And now when they left Plymouth they were driving directly to London for a conference.

He was standing outside the premises we were considering. The cold wind was biting into him, and he looked old and as frail as a leaf.

However the next time I saw him he was back to his old self.

When we return home from the Kings Bromley it is to find that the gossip about Ivor has subsided and things are returning to normal.

## 25

The only explanation I can offer for my decision to join the casino robbery gang is that with the death of Ivor the odds are a little less against us.

But I worry about the style of the raid. The Bluffer smuggled brandy and that had a certain elegance to it. By comparison what we are planning is very crude. But in the end the Bluffer would probably have given us his blessing, saying it reminded him of one of his cross channel commando raids.

There are regular planning meetings at the house. George gives us up to date reports on staffing levels and current cashing up processes and Jackie tells us about security and alarm systems. Mr Chong gives Supin lessons in firing positions and gun handling. Mr Chong is a puzzle. He is our armourer and he is training Supin, but he is adamant he will not go on the raid itself. He is the oldest of our group and has spent time in jail in Hong Kong. If we are caught and long sentences are given it is likely that he will die in prison.

As we made our plans I considered our motives.

There was my sister Alison's decision to plant those trees and create that little arboretum in Northern Ireland. Was that a conscious decision on her part or was she responding to something more primeval and instinctive?

There was also my mother and her pictures and their strangely differing styles. The nicely mannered water colours followed by the stick like riders on horseback and finally those last vivid acrylics.

And of course the Bluffer with his mad book and my walk across Europe.

How many people have looked at me and said well now why would you want to do that?

And I have looked back, unable to give any sort of coherent answer. If I had said that to feel the road under my feet day after day and to unfold a map and to see my slow snail like progress and to see new names emerge and to watch old names fade away is a sensation I am glad I have experienced, I know that would have elicited only a yawn and a nod of incomprehension.

So is that what it is all about? Are we simply trying to tell the world who we really are? Or is it a need to leave a mark or a trace behind?

Perhaps it is darker than that.

These robbers have all been battered about by life. They are angry. They are out for revenge. They want some of the good things as well. Supin concentrates as Mr Chong instructs her in the use of the pistol. She is about to take her revenge on a world that has given her Parkinson's disease. George and Jackie are also angry. I often thought at this time of Counterpart, the Bluffer's book.

It was George who organised our timetable. He told us we had to wait until there was the correct staff compliment on duty.

Then as we waited, our training all done, Supin and George turned their attention, of all strange things, to the construction of a doll's house.

Supin had told a Chinese woman who gambled at the casino that at one time she had built the kitchen cupboards for our house. So the Chinese woman had said in that case could she build a doll's house for her daughter's birthday?

So wood is bought and tools that have not been used in several years are brought up from the basement.

After that in the conservatory of our house, with George acting as her assistant, cigarette hanging from the side of his sad old mouth, the work begins.

During this period, the calm before the storm, the plan to rob the casino is put to one side.

Meals are taken as we work. All else is forgotten. Jackie and Mr Chong come round to the house to admire the construction. In the end it rises to such a height that I have to point out that if it gets any larger it will never get through the conservatory door.

Two days before the birthday it is completed and loaded into the car and delivered around to the house of the lady who has ordered it.

We heard afterwards that the daughter had been overwhelmed. It was certainly an astonishing creation for someone in Supin's condition.

But really there was nothing that Supin could not do with her hands. She cooked and gardened by instinct. She could make her own clothes and if she had any sort of training I am sure she could have been a good artist.

# 26

A week after the doll's house had been completed and delivered we made our robbery attempt.

We ate a light supper and then filed out of the house shortly after ten o'clock. I thought of the Bluffer setting off on one of his war time raids. I looked up at the sky and saw that it was dark and covered. I smiled to myself. That would have suited him. But whatever the weather, we would still need all our nerve.

Supin was next to me in the front and in her bag was the old pistol, fully loaded up with ammunition. George and Jackie were in the back.

None of us spoke as we set off into town. We were all nervous. As we descended down Mannamead toward Mutley a light rain began to fall and the road looked slick under the streetlights. Supins's face was set and pale.

She had dressed sensibly. Nothing too flashy. The bag to carry the gun was one she would use normally. Nothing to draw attention.

I parked in the Colin Campbell Court car park and Jackie got out and started walking toward the back entrance of the casino. Soon his thin figure had merged with the dark shadow of the building and I started up the car again.

We then did a slow circle around the Hoe and the Barbican, stopping briefly at Phoenix Wharf before we made our way back to the casino. The plan was for Supin and George to go in at a different time to Jackie. Again nothing to raise suspicion.

We got out of the car and I kissed Supin. Her face was determined as she leant toward me. Then she held my hand and said, 'Don't worry everything going to be alright.' I hoped it would be because she was a woman of great strength whom I loved deeply.

I watched as they disappeared into the darkness of the building. Supin was using a stick but aside from that she was walking as well I had seen her walk in months.

After that I moved off from the car park. I didn't want to be noted by any passing police car. I drove up on to the Hoe and parked there for a while.

How many times have I parked on the same spot since, looking out toward the Breakwater, to where we scattered Supin's ashes?

For a few moments I considered very sombrely what we had set in motion and of the consequences for all of us and for our families.

As we had planned the robbery we had discussed our roles. It was obvious to everyone that my job should be to drive the getaway car. But as I sat there on the Hoe that night I wondered whether Arthur Polianski, my fictional nemesis, would have accepted such a position. I am sure he would have insisted on leading the raiding party from the front.

So then I bought fish and chips and drove down to the Barbican and looked at the tied up fishing boats and waited.

Inside the casino the raiding party entered the gaming room.

Supin chose a table and played Blackjack for half an hour. She won a small amount at first but then lost three hands on the go. All normal, nothing suspicious. After that she got up and walked casually to a table by the far wall where there was a thick curtain.

Then she nodded to George who in turn engaged a croupier and a pit boss in conversation. This allowed her to slip un noticed behind the curtain into a small alcove where spare chairs and card tables were stacked. Within a few minutes she had been joined by George and Jackie.

During our planning sessions I had pointed out that at this moment of entry into the alcove the raiding party was at its most vulnerable.

Later I asked both George and Supin what was going through their minds as they sat in that little alcove. They had to wait nearly three hours and they hardly dared move for fear of alerting someone.

George said he had gone over the time during the war when as a child he had been evacuated from Liverpool to Wales. He said it had been the happiest time of his life. He said he dreaded going to prison. He had left enough clues slip for me to guess that he had done a spell inside when he was younger.

Supin said she wasn't afraid of going to prison at all. I quite believed her. When she had been receiving instruction from Mr Chong on use of the gun she had looked confident and determined.

Supin is like the Bluffer, she has all sorts of hidden depths.

In the same way that people did not believe that the Bluffer could have written a book such as Counterpart they also queried as to whether Supin would have had sufficient stamina and conviction to rob the casino.

My answer to that is that nobody knew Supin as well as I did. She always did exactly what she wanted. And she was never more determined than when she was angry. And right now she was angry with life for giving her Parkinson's disease and angry with the casino for taking her money.

As they waited there was one heart stopping moment when they heard a waitress shout out that more chairs were needed for a card game that was starting in a corner. They heard the waitress approaching the alcove but then at the last moment one of the managers called out countermanding the order.

Then in the early hours the croupiers called their final spins and the customers began to drift away. The three of them hardly dared breathe as they waited.

They could hear the manager and his two assistants talking. Then the last of the staff had gone and the boxes with the money were being brought to one of the Roulette tables. The counting would start soon.

It was at this point that the three of them pulled on their gloves and drew down the masks over their faces. Supin took the gun from her bag and pushed the safety switch to the off position. Later she said that she had been completely calm, not nervous at all. But George told me that just before they pulled down their masks he had glanced over at her and seen that her forehead was covered in sweat.

Then George gives the signal, Jackie yanks back the curtain and the three of them, that hobbledehoy gang, step out onto the gaming room floor.

It has all been planned precisely.

George yells out, 'Don't turn round, flat on the floor.' At the same time Supin drops into the brace position that Mr Chong has shown her, takes a deep breath, closes her eyes and fires a first shot into the ceiling.

Later all three of them all say that they are taken by surprise by the enormous sound the old gun makes as it fires. They say they can feel the shock wave ricocheting through them.

The three managers go face down on the floor immediately. But then one of them begins to move so Supin, she shows no hesitation now, fires a second shot into the ceiling. This procedure has been agreed beforehand.

Then Jackie is crouching over the three figures on the floor, handcuffing them quickly and expertly before pulling cloth bags over their heads.

Then as they have arranged they all stop to listen. They count slowly to five. But there is nothing. Dead silence.

Then Jackie runs quickly over to the reception desk and reaches underneath to switch off the alarm. After that he gets up on a chair and removes the cassette from the security video.

Then he is into the office removing the cassettes from the security cameras which cover the gaming room. All the time Supin is steady as a rock. She has positioned herself so that she can cover both the door and the three men on the floor.

During this period all the raiders maintain their discipline, none of them says a word.

George now tips all the bundles of notes and bags of coins along with the account books and till rolls for the evening into two thick black bin bags. Jackie adds the security camera tapes and the guest register from the office.

In training we had timed the robbery, start to finish, at five minutes, but when it is for real, with the adrenaline pumping, they do it in four.

The last act is for Jackie to release the handcuffs. George then tells the managers to keep their hoods on and not to move for five minutes if they value their lives. This again is a vulnerable moment. If the managers get up we could have a fight, but to the relief of the raiders they stay on the floor without moving.

Waiting in the car I have my hand on the key, straining to see into the shadows. Finally I spot the three figures, carrying the two black bin bags, coming toward me.

I rolled slowly up to meet them. When they were in nobody said a word, though I could hear their excited breathing as I drove carefully out of the car park. We made our way out of town but no one followed us. Soon we were through Mutley Plain and climbing up past Mannamead.

We were half a mile from the house and had been driving for ten minutes when finally Supin broke the silence and with a lovely low laugh said, 'Well, you know what, we done it.' Then Jackie began to laugh as well and a smile even crept across old George's face.

Then we pulled up in the driveway and got out of the car and went inside and spread all that lovely money all over the living room carpet.

Mr Chong served us at the table and we cracked open a bottle of champagne and drank to all our healths and to our future and to the success of the raid. After that we all complimented Mr Chong on his cuisine and declared it the best meal we had ever eaten. Then suddenly we were all chattering away telling our tales and Supin said she wasn't a bit tired at all.

When we had eaten we counted the money and George noted the figures in an account book. We were astonished at how much we had got. It was almost double what we had expected. George said it was possible that for some reason the previous night's takings had not been banked.

As the three robbers were sorting through the money and totalling it all up and Mr Chong was clearing up in the kitchen I took the gloves and the masks and tills rolls and registers and went out into the back garden and made a small bonfire and burned them.

Then I took the gun and all the ammunition that was left over and the plastic security videos and put them into a black bin bag, adding some stones from the garden.

After that, while the others were still talking about the raid, I drove back into town and stopped at Laira Bridge. There I dumped the bag over the side of the bridge and into the river and watched it sink.

As I drove slowly home I contemplated our future and wondered what it would bring for all of us. We may have been a hobbledehoy gang of no hopers but somehow we had pulled it off. Turning finally into the driveway and getting out of the car I noticed that the dawn was beginning to break.

# 27

After I left Kolasin I dipped down into a valley and then began a climb up a steep pass the other side. Once again I could see that the crests of the mountains all had snow on them. I camped out that night half way up the pass and the following day I reached Andrijevica and stayed a night in a hotel there.

The next morning the owner put my map out on the bar and told me he was sure that the crossing into Kosovo, directly to the West, had been re opened.

But as I walked along the road, noting the potholes and the lack of traffic, I began to doubt him. When after two hours I came to a small collection of houses and a road side shop my suspicions were confirmed. The border had been closed since the NATO bombing, so I was informed.

I hated to go back. There is nothing more discouraging than retracing footsteps.

So when the shop owner said that his brother would shortly be leaving for Rozaje I took the advantage of a lift and that is how I ended up fifty miles to the North West at the foot of the main pass leading into Kosovo.

For me a morning's walk might be a steady climb up of four or five hours and a view out over forests and mountains still covered with snow and then a descent back down again. On the whole things were pretty quiet.

The climb up from Rozaje was the exception. It was one of the main routes East and every ten or twenty minutes a bus or a heavy truck would grind its way up past me.

It was a tough enough hike and it took me almost twenty four hours to get to the frontier post at the top. I camped out by the side of the steep road. During the night I could still hear the heavy lorries as they went uncomfortably close past my tent.

There is not a book long enough to go into all of Balkan history. But as a summary: In 1998 terrible fighting broke out between Serbs and Kosovans. As a result hundreds of thousands of Kosovans were forced to flee, many taking to the woods and the mountains to escape.

A routard does not have the understanding of a country that a foreign correspondent has. In Kosovo I did not speak to any government ministers, or businessmen, or even, knowingly at least, to any of the mafia style gangsters that are supposed to thrive here.

But a routard, because he goes so slowly, does have the advantage of being able to study carefully what is directly before his eyes.

Nothing in Kosovo is that odd by itself. In that way it is similar to Northern Ireland. It is simply the accumulation of detail.

On the road south of Pec I was shocked by the number of small roadside cemeteries I came across. Where I could I checked dates and read inscriptions. On occasion all the dates were the same, indicating a massacre.

The largest grave I saw was outside Gjakova. As I approached I saw a sea of red flowers covering an area the size of several football pitches. There must have been hundreds of graves. But when I was up close, and this is an image that has stayed in my mind, I saw that all the flowers were plastic.

I was told that the war had left its mark on that generation of Kosovans in all sorts of strange ways. For example, thousands of Kosovan children were evacuated to other European countries to escape the Serbian invasion and now, in calmer times, many of them have returned. So now, as well as speaking Albanian, they are also comfortable in Swedish or Norwegian or Danish.

Since the end of the war there has been a great effort at reconstruction in Kosovo. Old houses are being torn down and new buildings are going up. I am sure by some economic indicators Kosovo is regarded as a dynamic society. But this has left all sorts of strange anomalies.

For instance as I walked I noted that there were certainly more car wash establishments than could be warranted by the amount of traffic on the roads. I have no idea whether these were the fad of the moment, or were being used to soak up government funds or to launder illicit money. Or perhaps there was another explanation.

There were two types of transport I saw, and they were at the opposing ends of the social scale. There were the peasant farmers going slowly along in donkey carts and there were the drivers of large Mercedes or Land Cruisers, with darkened windows and Albanian number plates, who overtook them at high speed. So maybe the reason for all the car washes is that the gangsters just liked to keep their cars clean.

One day I took a wrong turning and came to a small village with a garage. I laid out the map on the ground and went over it with the mechanic. In the end we worked out that it was the map that was wrong. The cartographer had included a road that did not exist.

Another type of tourist, going by car or bus, would have noticed other points. But these are the things that I came across as a walker.

I stayed in Pec, which was the first town I came into Kosovo, for several days. There a man who ran a cafe, interested in my travels, looked at my map and re traced the route he and his family had taken over the mountains to escape the Serbian soldiers who had been chasing them.

The stories he told me were horrible. Elderly people forced over the mountains without proper food or clothing. He said he had decided to come back but he had a brother who had settled permanently in London.

All this was happening long before I read Counterpart, the Bluffer's book. But now as I write this account I find myself thinking of the dark things the Bluffer wrote about. He makes reference to the Balkan wars of course, but he has concentrated, understandably, on the massacre at Srebrenica.

The wars in Kosovo have been over for more than ten years now and aside from the roadside graves I did not see any other outward signs of the horror. By contrast in Belfast, the two communities are still divided by a physical barrier.

But I have a feeling there are a lot of similarities.

There is the story everyone knows in Northern Ireland of how a group of drunken youths broke into the zoo in Belfast and rounded up the penguins. Then they attacked them with iron bars and threw as many as they could over the wall into the lions enclosure.

At the same time there have been allegations made that during the war Hashim Thaci, who became the Kosovan Prime Minister, was part of a group that took Serbian prisoners into Albania and shot them and then removed their organs and sold them.

Does the horror of war cause some sort of mutation in people's personalities? The Bluffer had a lot to say about that in his book.

A visitor from the Balkans staying in Northern Ireland would also discover a patchwork of allegiances every bit as obtuse as in the Balkans. Each town in Northern Ireland stills puts up the flags that indicate its loyalties.

The climb out of Prizren as I made my way further south was a long one. From the town to the top of the pass took me once again about twenty four hours. As I plodded slowly up I noted the number of large new houses, you could call them mansions, with swimming pools and heavily guarded gates.

But at the top the tree line has been left behind, the slopes are bare. The air is clean and fresh and it is possible to see for miles all around. Battered old trucks stop at the top and the drivers stretch their legs and eat at the roadside bars.

To the left I could see that some new houses were being built. I was told that these were holiday homes for government ministers and other important people. The air here was supposed to be especially good for health. It was called something like The Place Where The Four Winds Blow.

But on that sunny day on top of the pass sitting at a roadside cafe I ordered slices of lamb and chips and a bottle of beer. Fifty yards away cows sat on the grass being tended by women in headscarves, also sitting on the grass. The women seemed to be as large as the cows. If I could have stayed there in that state of mind, I would have been very happy.

The descent down the other side was a lesson in the strange political geography of that area because when I said good afternoon to a man in Albanian I was surprised to receive a reply in Serbian.

That evening I discovered that I had passed into a small Serbian enclave. There weren't more than a few hundred of them and they were very defensive of their position.

A day later, after spending a night in a cheap hotel where the window fell out when I tried to open it, I turned to the south and after going over once last pass I was in sight of Macedonia.

Then, that afternoon, in another roadside cafe I heard a man talking to his son in English and I could make out a strong Irish accent. So I went over and said hello and he told me that he had left Kosovo some years ago and had married an Irish girl and they now lived in the town of Wexford. I said that the Bluffer had lived for many years in County Donegal and that I had lived in Dublin with Supin and written for the Irish newspapers and so we swopped stories. I told him how beautiful Supin was but that now she suffered from Parkinson's disease.

He told me that he had been working as a builder and he and his wife had been given a council house in Wexford and everything had been going very well until he had hurt his back and had to go on the sick.

So I asked him how they were managing now and he said he was using his time off work in Ireland to help his brother build a house here in Kosovo.

He told me that the house was going to have six bedrooms and however many bathrooms and would do well for all the family.

The idea that by this roundabout route the Irish government was funding a house building programme in Kosovo seemed in keeping with the oddity of this small country. His son had been born in Ireland, spoke no Albanian and was anxious to go home.

After that I came to the Macedonian border. I was tired by then and it was getting dark so when a taxi driver said that, for a reasonable fee, he would take me into to Skopje I accepted and that is how I found myself staying at the Hotel Brams.

# 28

I was becoming seriously concerned for Supin's health.

Within weeks of the robbery she had begun to lose weight. Her clothes started to hang off her and she found it increasingly difficult to keep her balance. She had gone quickly from using a stick to needing the support of a frame.

The effort she had made during the robbery had exhausted her meagre reserves.

Then one afternoon she fell heavily as she got out of the car. A day later her left leg was bruised from knee to hip. She was shocked and in pain. The doctor told us she was lucky not to have a serious fracture.

After that, for most of the time until the operation, it was easier for her to use a wheelchair.

So that is the state she was in, quite feeble really, when one afternoon a month after the robbery the door bell rang. When I answered it I found two detectives standing there with some very serious questions to ask us.

After the robbery the casino had been closed up while forensic examinations were made. The bullets Supin had fired were dug out of the ceiling and matched to a type of gun.

But I had ditched the pistol over Laira Bridge and we had taken care to leave no other traces. Additionally because we had removed the registers and security cameras, these were the days before everything was available on line, it was difficult for the police to establish who had been in the casino that night.

In the end all the regulars had been interviewed. Two uniformed policemen came to the house to speak to us. But Mr Chong was our alibi. We had admitted to being at the casino but said we left early because we had asked Mr Chong to cook dinner for us. Supin was in her wheelchair during the interview and when they left we did not expect to hear anything more.

When Ivor was still alive I had ridiculed the robbery plan. But when we pulled it off I swung the other way. I convinced myself that somehow, perhaps due to the power of our great criminal minds, we had staged a perfect robbery.

Now it seemed I was wrong.

These detectives were different altogether from the two policemen who had interviewed us earlier. They declined my offer of tea. They had a new line of enquiry. They were interested in the car. They said there had been several sightings of an old Mondeo leaving the scene of the crime at about the right time.

As it happened, and all this is true, a week after the raid I had gone to Bristol in connection with an article I was writing. As I was coming back late at night I decided to take a short cut over Dartmoor via Princetown. There I ran into a Dartmoor pony that had strayed onto the road and wrote off the old Mondeo.

But when I recounted this story to the two detectives I could see the disbelief in their eyes. One of the detectives put down his notebook and stared at me. Later they traced the car to a scrap yard but by that time, in a piece of good fortune for us, it had already been broken up.

They even came back a third time, this time there was a woman officer with them. She spent half an hour trying to coax answers out of Supin but got nowhere. Afterward Supin said she had felt her heart beating at a hundred miles an hour.

They left us alone after that but I am sure they were still suspicious. But then George got a whisper that they were now working on the theory that it was an inside job and so that took the attention away from us.

## 29

A month after our last visit from the police we finally received the date for Supin's operation at Frenchay Hospital in Bristol.

In my opinion the operation came just in time.

This was because the Parkinson's disease, despite all her valiant efforts, was finally getting the better of her. After so many years she was slowly sinking beneath the weight of it all.

I have already described how she was losing weight but now she was fading away before my eyes. This was because her arms and legs were constantly moving. This is what the doctors call involuntary dyskinesia.

She used to say she did a ten mile run every day, without even leaving the house. This constant movement, which was partially a side effect of the medication she was taking, left her exhausted.

And Mr Parkinson, who was so rotten and malign, was also catching her another way. The constant movement was now also making it difficult to eat. The simple act of lifting fork to mouth without spilling food was a battle. In the later stages of Parkinson's disease swallowing also becomes a problem.

However if I have painted a dark picture here there were still good moments.

Supin said she felt like the Queen of Thailand when I pushed her round in the wheelchair. I responded that I was happy to be her humble slave.

We also replayed the detail of the robbery. She loved telling me how she had fired the shots into the ceiling.

Our financial difficulties were also certainly over. We were soon able to sell up in Plymouth and move to our new little house in Cornwall.

I recall the drive up to Bristol for the operation. We left very early that clear summer's morning. As we set off the sky was still red with the dawn.

We had replaced the Mondeo with a silver Peugeot. We could have afforded something grander but that would have drawn attention to ourselves. Our only luxury was to make it an automatic. This would make it easier for Supin if she wanted to drive again.

We made our way up the old familiar route. The A38 past Ashburton to Haldon Hills, then the M5 passing Exeter, Taunton and on toward Bristol.

Supin is tired that morning, she is always tired these days. I glance across and see that her eyes are closed. But in our own way we are both quite happy. We are optimistic. We are still gamblers. We are sure that the operation is our wild card, our joker, that is going to get us out of all this.

We pass Taunton and she wakes up and leans forward and pushes a CD into the player. She has a new favourite every day but in the end we always come back to Patsy Cline. She loves that voice. It's jaunty, funny, melancholic.

When we were selecting the music to play for the funeral service the first song I chose, thinking of that morning, was by Patsy Cline.

In the original Thai version of her memoir there is a detailed description of the operation but for some reason when it was translated into English this was left out.

Our surgeon was Mr Steven Gill. He was assisted by Dr Peter Heywood and our Parkinson's specialist nurse was Karen O'Sullivan. It all happened many years now but I still offer you my heartfelt thanks.

What those brilliant surgeons and nurses did was to lift the top off Supin's head, while she was still conscious. They then carefully drilled down, making space to insert two electrical wires at the point of the brain where the problem lay. The wires were then hooked up to a battery which was inserted in the chest. This battery gives off a tiny electrical stimulus. The operation is known as Deep Brain Stimulation and is now widely used both for Parkinson's disease and other problems. The main benefit for Supin, and I can only report on what I observed, was that it allowed her to halve the amount of Sinemet she had been taking. This in turn reduced the dyskinesia, the involuntary movements. Within weeks, to my eyes, she was a different woman. By some miracle, or so it seemed to us, we had turned back the clock.

# 30

I quickly found myself becoming a citizen of Skopje.

I took the bus into the centre in the morning and nosed around. I went to an internet cafe and corresponded uncomfortably with the Bluffer and received news of Supin.

One day to my delight I discovered a Chinese restaurant and ordered spring rolls followed by noodles with seafood. When the spring rolls arrived and they were just the wrapping and nothing else I let it pass but when the main course came and it turned out to be spaghetti with a packet of frozen prawns added I had to say something.

So I called over the waitress, I was the only person in the restaurant, who in turn called the Chinese manageress, or she may have been the owner, who explained that was the way the Macedonians liked to eat their Chinese food.

When I said, quite sharply, that I did not believe her she looked completely astonished. But in the end I ate up and paid up but on the way out I looked into the kitchen and saw that the cook certainly was not Chinese.

I always felt happy when I went home on the old rattle trap bus with the exhaust fumes puffing out of the back. I felt as sleepy and tired as the other passengers, though my tiredness was due to good wine and good Macedonian food rather than the result of having worked a twelve hour shift. That is my main memory of Skopje, the tiredness of the people on the late night bus as we went home.

Then one morning, going in on the bus, a woman of about thirty approached me. She had seen that I was a foreigner and she wanted to talk. I told her something of my travels and how I was planning to walk as far as Istanbul. She said that she was a teacher and that she had a group of students who were learning English at night school, so that evening I was invited to address them.

The evening was not a success. The students were trying to improve their English so that they could go abroad, preferably to America. They were mystified, and quickly uninterested, as to why someone should want to walk if they could afford a car. Their questions were all about jobs and pay levels and prospects in England and America. Almost all of these questions I was unable to answer.

I left the class discouraged and went to a bar where I was used to drinking a late night beer. In the corner was a computer for the use of clients and I switched it on but there were no email messages for me so I turned to the news web sites.

There I read that in Rome there had been a bizarre attempt on the life of the Pope.

I put down my drink and began to pay attention when I read that the assassin, who had been in the crowd in St Peter's Square as the Pope was giving an address, had fired a bolt from what was described as a home made crossbow.

I scrolled the report down further.

An eye witness was saying that the assassin had been jostled as he was taking aim and that the bolt had flown wide striking a cardinal who had been standing next to the Pope. But according to the doctors at the hospital where the Cardinal was taken the wound was only superficial.

As it had happened in the last twelve hours the assassin had not been yet been named.

I switched off the computer and ordered a glass of whiskey and went outside in the warm night to take a seat and smoke a cigarette and consider the situation.

Vilis had certainly said that art should be revolutionary if it was to have a purpose but I had no idea he meant anything as drastic as that.

I had no great love for the Pope but I was still shocked by this turn of events.

Finally I raised a glass to him.

'Here's to you Vilis old boy,' I said out loud.

I hoped that his revolutionary heroes old Tom Paine and the poet Shelley would be proud of him.

Then I began to think about the person who had nudged his shoulder and ruined his aim. Had the shot that should have rung out across the world been averted by someone blowing their nose?

Then I felt quickly discouraged. I hoped that Vilis was prepared. They would bury him alive for what he had done.

Just then one of the students from the class walked by the bar on her way home and she spotted me and I invited her to join me for a drink.

She had heard that there had been an attempt on the life of the Pope, her family was Catholic, and she wanted to know my opinion on it.

For a moment I was completely stumped. I wanted to tell her, she was very pretty and I am sure she would have been impressed and one thing might have led to another, that I knew Vilis.

But I stopped myself. I did not want her calling the police to say that the accomplice of the mad man who had tried to kill the Pope was right here in Skopje.

So I drew a deep breath and said it was certainly a sad moment but that it was a lucky escape for the Pope and that the man who tried to kill him was certainly mad. This seemed to satisfy her, it was what she wanted to hear, and she got up a few minutes later and said she had to go home.

After that I sat for a long time thinking about this and that and wondering if I had betrayed Vilis. He had the courage of his convictions and was prepared to act. He was not afraid to be martyred. Would his hero Shelley have betrayed him like that? Going home on the bus that night I decided I was a coward.

The next day I went to an internet cafe across the square from the hotel. There was more information on the attempted assassination. It was headline news all over the world. Vilis had now been identified. But he had laid his plans well.

A web site based in Latvia had released a call to arms that he had written. It was short and succinct and contained extracts from the Mask of Anarchy. It would certainly be difficult to call it the work of a mad man. I read it a couple of times and thought he had done an excellent job.

I had to smile a few days later when I heard that at a demonstration by a group of anarchists in America in support of Vilis they had been heard to chant, 'Ye are Many, They are Few.'

Two days later, my head still full of Vilis and his extraordinary act I bade farewell to the city of Skopje. I went, as usual, by the smaller roads, following as much as I could the course of the River Vardar in a direction that went south west toward the Greek border.

The sense of life re seeding itself in Kosovo seemed to me to be largely absent in Macedonia. A lot of people wanted to emigrate and many had already gone. This gave the country a somnolent air.

To the north of the town of Veles the road passed by a lake where a large boat, really a floating hotel, was moored. I spent a couple of days there. One night there was a wedding party and I was invited to join in and drank too much.

Sometime after that I reached the town of Gevgelija which is on the border with Greece. Like a lot of border towns it has its own dynamic. Wikipedia states that it has a population of just fifteen thousand but it also has at least five large casinos.

At that time it was the Greeks coming across the border to play in the casinos. All that has probably changed now.

But anyhow I got a room in a cheap hotel across the street from one of the casinos and in the evening after I had scrubbed up as best as I could I entered the casino to find, as I hoped, that there was the usual free buffet. It seems that casinos are the same the world over.

I stayed in Gevgelija for three days eating at the casino and watching the gamblers and thinking of Supin. I had a problem with a foot, a series of blisters had appeared, and I wanted to give it a chance to heel. During the day I read and wondered around the town and also thought of Vilis and hoped that he wasn't getting too hard a time in prison.

After that I went down into Greece to Thessalonika but finding it too expensive and a throw back to the old

Europe I had left behind I turned back north again and via the town of Serres crossed the border into Bulgaria.

There I passed through the Western Rhodope Mountains and the towns of Gotse Delchev, Dospat, Smolyan and Kardzali. The mountains were high, clear and beautiful and I felt very at home there.

In one village I was given a room in a half finished hotel. It was far too large for the village it was in. It was also obvious that no work had gone on there for a long time. It could have been abandoned when the Communist regime fell. I was certainly the only guest. As I walked around I wondered if any other guests had ever stayed there. There was a dining room but it was full of building materials. The door of my room had a leather covering but the walls were bare concrete and there was dust everywhere. But there was an iron bed with a mattress and blankets piled up on it, so it seemed it had been used by someone.

In the evening I stood on the balcony and watched the farmers coming in from the fields. They were riding in small covered wagons pulled by horses or donkeys. Tobacco was the crop here. I counted at least thirty wagons coming in, all in good condition, the shoes of the horses clip clopping on the road as they came up. Because there was nowhere to eat I set up my camping gas stove on the balcony and cooked up hot dogs and noodles and drank beer and watched those horses and wagons returning to the backdrop of the setting sun.

I am sure I could live in the Rhodope Mountains.

Days later dropping down the steep road in to Smolyan I saw in the distance a tall tower block, it must have been a dozen storeys high. I tried to imagine why someone should have built such a tall and imposing building in such a rural setting. When I drew near and eventually passed the building, which was on the outskirts of the town, I saw that it was in fact abandoned. A couple of burned out cars and some bags of building rubble were standing in front of it. So I walked on and then something made me turn my head and I looked back and saw the words hotel written on the front.

In all my travels this is the hotel for which I have the most affection.

The building was at least a dozen storeys high but only the lowest three storeys were functional. It was difficult to know which way it was going. Was it being abandoned, floor by floor, or conversely was it being restored slowly upwards? When I look back now, I am sure it was the latter. But at that time the lift did not work because there were no cables. The restaurant was closed and the door to it bolted. The reception area was enormous and done out in a sort of marble but the lighting was dim so it was like being in perpetual twilight. Every day there was a different girl on the reception and they were always friendly.

My room on the third floor had a balcony over looking the valley and the town. It felt like a ship's cabin. The walls were wood panelled and it was cosy and snug and clean. There was even hot water. I spent days on the balcony reading and looking out over the valley. In the evening I watched the football on the Eurosport with the night watchman. He spoke some English and I told him about the Bluffer and Supin and everything that had happened to me and he told me how he had spent two years in America with his daughter but had come home to Smolyan because he preferred it here. Over the valley I watched the sunshine playing on the leaves of the silver birch trees. I asked him what it was like in winter here in the snow and he said as good as in the summer.

Then one evening I came downstairs to see if there was anything on the television that night and he turned to me and said 'Well there is another one of you guys here tonight, another hiker. Pack on his back.' He tapped his shoulder to emphasise the point. 'Arrived an hour ago. Said he was going to come down later to watch the football.'

So then I got up and looked around and was amazed and delighted to see coming down the stairs my old friend and revolutionary Vilis Balodis.

# 31

They kept Supin in Frenchay Hospital for just over a week.

After the operation I sat by her bed and looked at her bruised and battered face. Her eyes were closed and she was sleeping gently.

Then finally she opened her eyes and looked around the ward. She was like a child waking up from a long sleep. To begin with she hadn't the slightest idea where she was.

She smiled as best she could out of her lopsided face and then reached out and took my hand.

Her first words were, ' I done alright or not?' To which I replied, ' Of course. You've done brilliantly,' and squeezed her hand.

Later we walked up and down the ward together and then she sat in a chair by the side of the bed.

When I got her home she was still very weak but I knew things were improving when I heard her on the telephone to the hairdresser asking her to come round to the house.

When she found her legs again and when the weather was warm enough she ventured out into the garden, we were then in our new house by the sea in Cornwall, and soon she was able to walk easily with just a stick.

Before the operation it had been frame and then wheelchair. Now she would go round the garden inspecting the flowers and looking out over the fields. Because the dyskinesia had subsided eating was easier and so the weight started to go back on.

On one occasion she even came with us on the steep path down to the beach. It was a Sunday afternoon and we had a picnic. It was as if we had wound back the clock.

She talked about all sorts of things then. She said that during the operation it felt like she was sitting in a dentist's chair. Now she was home she planned to work in the garden and pick berries and make jam and do all sorts of other things. She was even going to make another doll's house.

Then I remember the way she looked at me and said, 'I going to make up for all the time I lost.'

I often dream of that now, of winding back the clock. On occasion I replay that first opening scene. We go up to see John Gibson and instead of giving the verdict he does, he shakes his head and smiles and says, 'No don't worry, that's nothing, just carry on.'

Several weeks after we had returned home I woke in the middle of the night. I could hear Supin breathing beside me. It was then that certain things fell into place.

I had been puzzled as to why the three managers in the casino that Jackie had tied up and hooded did not recognise George's voice when he shouted out.

All the staff in the casino knew him and his Liverpool accent stood out. He had also picked a night when there was a lot more money than usual in the casino.

So as I lay there, the moonlight coming in through the window, I realised that it could have been an inside job actually set up by George. It was he who had filled up the bags with the money. Had he had left an extra bag behind for the manager and his assistants?

But I never said anything to Supin and I never said anything to George.

Jackie, as far as we were aware left Plymouth immediately for London with his share of the money and we never saw him again, though we heard that he had lost heavily at the casino in Leicester Square.

Then six months later George had a stroke and we went to visit him in Derriford Hospital. It is possible that John Gibson would have gone past him in the hospital though neither of them would have realised in what strange way they were connected.

We went in most days. He was finding it difficult to talk so we would discover him propped up on a pillow his head in a detective story. He said he had no regrets. He had lived his life. One day I remember he put the book he was reading to one side and said to me, a little smile on his face, ' We could tell a better story than that couldn't we?'

Two weeks later he had another stroke and died. There were half a dozen of us squeezed into suits at the funeral and then we stood by the graveside, on a cold grey day, mourning the passing of a good friend.

When we went to the hospital to pick up his things the nurse gave us a note he had left. This said that because we had always looked after him we were to have his share of the money which was under his bed at the house in Cattedown.

This left us with a dilemma. When we added George's share of the money to our own we had a lot of money. If we banked it in the normal way it would cause suspicion.

So one evening when we were at home and wondering what we were going to do about that I decided to ring the Bluffer.

On serious subjects such as money it's better to talk in an indirect manner with the Bluffer. I don't suppose for a moment anyone was listening in to his phone, perhaps it was a left over from war time caution.

So I said I had a certain proposition for him and then began to talk about strokes of good fortune and needs for safe havens.

There was a pause and I could hear him considering and decoding my proposition. He would have worked it out very quickly. He followed all the news. He knew we were gamblers and he would have read all about the robbery which had been reported in the national press.

After a moment he said, 'Tell me, the operation, you said it was a success. Can Supin travel yet?'

So I looked across at her. She was sitting on the sofa. The TV was on quietly in the corner and her eyes were half closed. I thought for a moment.

'Give it a few weeks more and she will be fine.'

'That's all I need to know,' said the Bluffer. 'I'll be in contact.'

And that's how it was with the Bluffer.

A month later we flew to Zurich and our hand luggage was certainly more precious than the hand luggage of any of the other passengers.

We met the Bluffer in the hotel he had booked us into and after that we took a taxi to the bank.

When he was close up to money the Bluffer became a different man. All the piss and wind disappeared.

He was dressed soberly in dark suit and white shirt and in the office of his man Peter Albrecht he was firm, direct and clever. Albrecht, also silver haired, listened gravely, occasionally nodding his head, as the Bluffer described what he wanted.

Incidentally, though Peter Albrecht always did well for us, two years later he fell down the stairs at his home outside the city and broke his neck.

Supin told me afterwards that as the Bluffer was speaking she had been looking round the sombre wood panelled office. She had been thinking about everything that had happened in her life.

She said that her mother and father, who had been poor farmers, would have been astonished to see her in Switzerland with all that money.

I replied that even Mr Thamnong, the Deputy Minister for Co operatives and Agriculture, would have been pretty damned impressed.

As she put her signature to the papers to open up our account I also thought that a lot of water had passed under the bridge to get us here.

There was the little wooden house where we had lived in Bangkok. There was our dog Duk. Then I remembered the astonishment of our neighbours when I bought that two ring electric stove.

That evening Supin and I stood the Bluffer an excellent meal at one of the best restaurants in Zurich. We talked about many things. Supin recounted the detail of her operation. I asked what my mother was painting at the moment and about Alison and her family. After that we made arrangements to go over and visit shortly.

Of course the Bluffer dropped little hints that he knew exactly how we had come by the money. He had his spies everywhere and would have had all the detail.

But for once in our life we were dining at the top table and we felt very content.

# 32

Vilis looked very thin after his ordeal. His face had sunk and when he smiled I could see a front tooth was missing.

I said I had been in Smolyan several days and knew a restaurant where it was possible to eat well. We dined outside and he took me through the dramatic events in St Peter's Square.

He had entered the square with the rest of the crowd, his cross bow hidden under his coat. He had positioned himself correctly. Then he had unbuttoned his coat and lifted up the crossbow to take aim and fire, he had practised a lot and could do it very quickly, when a woman standing next to him suddenly gave a violent sneeze and jogged his arm. As a result the bolt flew off to the left striking the cardinal on the arm instead.

So I had been right. His plan had been foiled by a random act.

As we ate Vilis told me about the police station where he had been taken. He had imagined it would be dark and sinister but it had been the opposite.

It had been brightly lit and flash guns had kept going off as people crowded around to take his picture. He had felt like a celebrity. His interrogation had been equally haphazard and chaotic. They had fed him well and even allowed journalists to interview him. Then after a few days he had been moved to an ordinary prison to await his trial.

We had finished eating by now and pushed away our plates and ordered more beers. I asked him how had he got out of jail. I had been watching him over dinner and thought for a moment he might be a double. But really there was no doubt that it was him.

So then he explained that it had been because of Vatican politics. The cardinal he had struck with the cross bow bolt was a great rival of the cardinal involved in his case. And as the injured cardinal had now decided to retire this made room for the cardinal involved in his case to advance.

Vilis said he had spent many hours talking to this cardinal and they had formed a friendship. Vilis had explained his political views and told him about Tom Paine and Shelley and how they were believers in democracy and equality and against hierarchies and despots and how he was planning to use their works as a defence at his trial. He said that he had chosen the Pope as a symbolic figure. Vilis said the cardinal must have been impressed by what he said because one night a guard had come into his cell and had given him back his old clothes. Then he had taken him out to the edge of the city and told him to be on his way.

I looked at him when he had concluded. He had followed a similar route to me. When he had crossed Italy he had taken the boat from Bari to Dubrovnik and worked his way slowly through Montenegro and Kosovo as I had. But in Macedonia he had turned East going straight into Bulgaria and avoiding Greece.

Back in the hotel he showed me his latest sketches. They were detailed images of people he had met on the way. I could see they were fine quality work. His plan was to continue on to Istanbul. There he hoped to put together a collection of the sketches and see if he could get a publisher interested in them.

We stayed another couple of days in Smolyan and then he went on ahead of me and we agreed to meet up again in Istanbul.

My next stop was in the town of Kardzali which is an extremely ugly place. A line of old tower blocks standing in a rough semi circle on a river bank has the appearance of a set of crumbling teeth in a giant's mouth. Unaccountably the two hotels in the centre of town were very expensive. So I took a taxi to a lake side resort five miles out of town and got a room in a wooden lodge overlooking the water. I stayed there in great comfort for several days before moving on once again.

Then finally I was in Edirne in Turkey and turning at last to face in the direction of Istanbul. The road down to Corlu was open and stinking hot. I passed a gang of road workers operating a tarmac laying machine and they ran after me to give me a bottle of water to drink. I stayed a night in a disgusting hotel in Corlu where the sheets were soiled and the mosquitoes buzzed.

By the time I reached Silvri and saw in front of me the Sea of Marmara that was enough. This was already the outskirts of the city. I regret it now. I wish I had gone on to the bitter end. But at the time I did not have the courage to do the last thirty miles through motorway links and industrial parks and flyovers and junctions. So I hopped on a bus and in an hour there I was in the centre of Istanbul. I stayed at the Cordial House Hotel in Sultanhamet which was cheapest place I could find.

The first night I ate dinner on a rooftop restaurant over looking the Bosphorus. If I turned my head to the right I could see the Blue Mosque and Hagia Sophia. Then I took out of my wallet the card from the Pensao Franca in Porto where I had stayed the night before beginning my walk. I laid it on the table in front of me and thought of the blue of the River Douro and the red tiles of the roofs of that city. It had certainly been a long time since I left there. I asked a waiter to record the moment on my camera and then wished I had someone to share it with.

Vilis arrived two days later with the story of an adventure that had befallen him in the town of Luleburgaz which is about fifty miles south east of Edirne. I smiled when I heard that name because I had observed a strange scene there myself.

I had woken in the middle of the night in my hotel room. Then I had looked down on to the silent empty street to see a pack of twenty big dogs running along. They were all black except the lead dog which was brindled and heavier than the others. This was one of the main streets of the town and when I looked it up in Wikipedia I saw that Luleburgaz has a population of a hundred thousand people.

Vilis's adventure had been different. In the centre of the town he had discovered an exhibition of art. As he had been looking at the paintings he had fallen into conversation with one of the artists, who he described as ravishingly beautiful. When he said he was also an artist and when she saw his sketches she was so overwhelmed she fell immediately in love with him. It was then that he told me, with some considerable excitement, she would arrive in Istanbul tomorrow.

So the next day when Cennet had made her entrance we took a cruise on the Bosphorous and ate at a small fish restaurant on the Asian side. She wasn't as I imagined. Vilis, in his excitement at finding someone who wanted him, he was really just an outcast, one grade above a tramp, had described her as an outstanding beauty. Actually she was skinny and gnarled and probably considerably older than he was. I am sure that Vilis was the better artist as well, but despite that, it was obvious that they were well suited.

We tramped all over the city. We walked along the Golden Horn, we rode back and forth on the ferries, we even found the house where the writer Orhan Pamuk lived. Vilis said he was a man of great courage because he had stood up to the government, but over lunch I said that Vilis was a man of probably greater courage. Cennet nodded violently at this and fell a bit more in love with him.

Then Vilis talked about the day he loaded up his rucksack and left Riga and I told a similar story of leaving Porto. I waited for Vilis to bring up the story of his attempt to assassinate the Pope but it was never mentioned. He had confined that to another time, and now he was beginning a new life with Cennet.

After that we talked about the future.

We talked endlessly of where we would go and what we would see and new horizons we would discover. Vilis said he could not get the name of Samarkand off his lips and I smiled when I heard that too.

But when we parted that was the last I heard of Vilis Balodis.

# 33

The day we first met Num, the journalist and photographer, I was part of a team at the Thai Buddhavihara temple in Kings Bromley, Staffordshire, that was pulling and heaving to raise a giant marquee in the garden.

It was a week when Phra Maha Laow was bustling energetically around, billowing his cape, issuing instructions to all, so that the whole temple was buzzing.

This was a good time for us. The robbery had given us back our financial stability and Supin was feeling the benefits of the operation.

The Bluffer and my mother, who were always attracted to old houses, would have loved this place. It is a grand three storey country house. Red brick, extensive gardens, gravel driveway, fish pond, stables. The Chanting Room with all the Buddha images is at the rear of the house.

I can see the Bluffer standing outside on the lawn. He is looking up, checking roofs, brickwork, measuring up with his eye, considering conversion possibilities. Then he turns to my mother, who is by his side, to say, ' You know my dear I think we could do something with this' and my mother nods in silent agreement. She can see the possibilities as well.

That is how I imagine the scene anyway. They were baffled when we moved to our small wooden house by the sea in Cornwall. It was not that they were against it, they simply could not understand it.

As we drove up to the temple I had been anticipating the moment when I would turn the handle on the front door and step inside.

It is similar to the first step a routard takes. The night before I started my walk across Europe I stayed at the Pensao Franca in Porto. In the morning I hesitated a long time before I picked up my pack knowing that it was the start of a long journey.

So it is on entering the temple.

I could always hear the silence as I took that first step across the threshold. Supin could hear it too. It's a special silence. It isn't the cold silence of an empty space. It's the opposite. It's a comforting silence, a warm silence, a silence that you can very nearly wrap around you. There is a smell of incense and a faint murmur of voices from the kitchen. I always just stand there and take a deep breath and think that for the next little while all our troubles are over.

The temple rises early. After prayers the monks, in their brown robes and with their heads shaven, file into the big kitchen for breakfast. Their numbers can vary but there are generally about half a dozen of them.

Thai people have a reputation for being shy and retiring but actually this is wrong. They are really very earthy and always laughing. Supin translated some of the jokes the monks told in the kitchen over meal times and I was surprised at how rude they were.

But today we are all flat out. Supin is working in the kitchen with the others and none of us is allowed to rest until all the preparations for the weekend fund raising fete are complete.

There is no one who can raise funds like Phra Maha Laow.

When he sold up the previous premises in Birmingham he borrowed heavily to move to Kings Bromley. But now with these fund raising fetes, the Thai community is astonishingly generous, most of the money has already been paid back.

But this fete is going to be a big one. We are expecting well over five hundred people and the Thai ambassador will be our guest of honour, so we have to put on a good show.

It was lunchtime before we finished. The last guy rope had been stretched and the last peg had been hammered in. It was then that I saw that Phra Maha Laow was talking to a journalist.

Phra Maha Laow loved being interviewed. Years ago, not long after he had arrived in this country and while he was still at the Buddhapadipa temple in Wimbledon, I wrote two long pieces about him, recounting his life thus far, for the Bangkok Post.

Num, the journalist, was holding out a microphone. Phra Maha Laow was speaking well in both Thai and English. When he had finished and Num had taken some pictures I went up to join them.

Num who was tall for a Thai had the same rather absent look that used to concern people about Jackie. But all other resemblance to Jackie ended there. Num ran a small Thai language journal in London.

The day was sunny and we ate our lunch together outside. Supin was busy with the others in the kitchen preparing for the fete.

Since the operation we have had several conversations about a project that Supin has been planning. She says she has been thinking about for it a long time. She is going to ask Phra Maha Laow if he will found a small temple in Plymouth. Since our arrival in Kings Bromley she has spoken to him about it several times and I know he is favourable. It will be a simple affair. To begin with it will be just a rented house where a Thai monk can come and live.

But as we ate that sunny lunchtime I told Num, 'If you are looking for a good story for your magazine you should speak to Supin.'

I then gave him a brief outline of everything that had happened with the Parkinson's disease and the operation and so on. Though of course I omitted all mention of the robbery and that side of our lives.

I could see he was very interested in this. But nothing could be done until the fete was out of the way.

On the day of the fete, which Phra Maha Laow later declared a great success, I supervised the car park while Supin had a seat at a table in the main marquee where she sold tickets for the raffle.

Supin's health was greatly improved after the operation but she still tired easily. I think in our happiness at the change in her we had forgotten that she was still very frail and that all we had really done was buy ourselves a little extra time.

When I went into the marquee I saw that her eyes were closing and that she was on the point of dropping off. I said, 'hello' and she jerked awake and looked at me. For a moment she had no idea who I was. After that I asked one of the other Thai women who was nearby to come and help her.

That incident reminded me of the time, some years ago now, when we were at the Bluffers and she had actually fallen asleep as we were eating dinner. She must have been dreaming because when she suddenly jerked back awake she turned to the Bluffer and asked in a loud voice if she could have a bath. Even the Bluffer was taken aback by that one, he had had been in full flow at the time, but he soon recovered.

It is early the following week that Supin begins to recount her story to Num.

At this point the temple was very quiet. Phra Maha Laow and his monks had turned to other duties, so in the afternoons I was free to go for long walks in the countryside.

I found the tow path next to the Trent and Mersey Canal and walked miles along it watching the barges as they went past.

Once, it was a long time ago now, we had thought of buying a barge and going to live on the canals.

But when I stopped and watched the people working their way up through the locks I realised how far that dream was away now.

Evening prayers are chanted in front of the Buddha image in the Chanting Room.

I loved in when it was dark outside and all the lights were turned off and the room was lit only by candles. Phra Maha Laow, kneeling on the floor in front of the main Buddha image, leads the chanting in his strong voice.

Supin and the others come into the Chanting Room. She leaves her stick at the edge of the room and comes in on all fours.

On those occasions I thought of the Bluffer and that strange book Counterpart that he wrote.

He had intended it, in part, to show the symmetry of the world. He knew, because he loved his garden, how all the plants had a symmetry to them that was mathematical in its precision.

So it occurred to me, as I sat there in the candlelight, that there was a sort of symmetry here as well. Phra Maha Laow, kneeling, palms together, was obviously mirroring the image of the golden Buddha in front of him.

To my ear the chanting was also intensely symmetrical, with patterns and motifs being constantly repeated.

But what was it that everyone believed? I have no idea. The meeting rooms were full of Buddhist tomes but I never saw anyone reading them. In all the years we went to Kings Bromley and other temples, I could always feel the calm, but the words, the theological terms and explanations, never meant anything to me.

My guess is that what we all took from it was the sense of a pattern, a sense of regularity, a sense of collectiveness and belonging, a sense that in this small world of the temple, for a brief moment, everything made sense.

The only small pebble in the shoe, which in the end caused considerable discomfort, were the activities of the immigration authorities. The world of the temple was beyond their comprehension.

On one occasion, so I was told, three officers from three different departments arrived at the same time to examine the papers and passports of the monks and guests. The people who were present said that the officers were openly hostile with their questioning.

As a result the monks now have to keep a log of all their movements as they go around the country. There is also a register kept in the temple which all visitors have to sign. Details of residence and nationality and immigration status all have to be recorded.

What was going through the minds of these officials as they made their investigations? What were they thinking as they entered the temple, their briefcases full of official documents? As they took off their shoes in the hallway and breathed in the faint scent of incense were they aware of the strangeness of their actions?

Would these people have merited a place in the Bluffer's book? Perhaps I am exaggerating their importance but at the time they did seem to me to be the antithesis of all that was light and good about the temple.

Num published the article about Supin, in Thai, in his journal the following month and after that it was translated into English by Pi Bhatsakhorn, one of the monks at the temple.

After that I did a further edit, adding some sections and altering some of the emphasis.

Then along with several new photographs it was printed in English in the magazine which Phra Maha Laow published from the temple. This is a magazine that is widely read among the Thai community in Britain.

I have a copy of the memoir on the table beside me as I write this now.

We also included it in the service sheet for the funeral. This is the first time that I have read it since the funeral and it has been an uncomfortable experience.

I regret that I did not take more note at the time of what Supin wrote.

When someone, whether it be my mother, or Alison my sister, or Supin, has such an impulse to express themselves, then not to take them seriously is to do them a disservice.

I hope in writing this short account I can rectify this.

Supin talks clearly about not giving up hope and how she overcame despair. She also talks of her pride at her three daughters all graduating from university.

Then there is a lovely phrase she uses. She says: ' I think life has a lot of miracles.'

That is a phrase that is still ringing through my head as I go for my walk this afternoon along the Cornish cliff top. Sometimes the wind here is so strong here that it is impossible to walk directly into it. Today the tide has covered over the beach and there are white waves thundering onto the rocks below.

The publication of the article marked a turning point for Supin in many ways. People would visit or telephone the house and she would talk to them about what she had learned from Phra Maha Laow. She also talked to them about the idea she had to found a Thai temple for the people of our area. The time when we had robbed the casino now seemed part of another life.

# 34

The Bluffer and my mother are settled at Ballyarr in the Irish Republic. The hotel in Wales has been sold several years before.

The Bluffer has spent the middle weekend of that August at Les Valettes. He and Edward have made an excursion by car to Geneva where they have dined at a very good restaurant and then stayed up late into the night drinking.

Then on the Monday morning he takes the plane from Nice to Heathrow where he changes and gets the British Airways flight to Belfast. He collects his car which he had left in the airport car park. When he thought about it afterwards he realised he could have been picked up and followed at any time during his stay at Les Valettes. That evening he stayed with Mac in Belfast. It was then that Mac told him that the security situation was getting more difficult, ' by the day' and that he had gone as far as wearing a pistol in court under his robes. When the Bluffer discussed it with my mother later he described Mac as being in, ' rather sombre sort of mood.'

Then on the Tuesday morning he set off on the two and a half hour drive from Belfast to home. The route, which he had driven many times before, would take him via Antrim over the Glenshane pass, through the centre of Derry and then past the customs post at Killea and on into the Irish Republic until he finally arrived back at Ballyarr.

What was the Bluffer thinking as he set off that morning? He was certainly tired and looking forward to getting home. He would have wanted to see my mother and tell her of his adventures and give her the latest gossip about Edward. Then he would have been glad to get back to his normal routine. He loved to cut the grass and walk around his grounds examining things.

The Bluffer has an excellent memory. He is on a straight stretch of road ten miles before Randalstown and there is a gap of about a hundred yards to the next car ahead of him. He remembers it as a dark coloured Volkswagen Beetle. Coming in the opposite direction is a small van. Then just as the van passes him and with the gap holding steady to the VW, three men in military uniform, he presumes it as an army patrol, step out into the road and wave him down. The Bluffer is forced to break hard to stop in time. That is why I consider that morning the Bluffer was either tired or distracted. Maybe he had not slept well, maybe he was thinking of home, maybe he was considering some new business venture that Edward had proposed, maybe he had leaned forward to turn on the radio, or maybe he was thinking about the warning that Mac had given him.

A Bluffer who had been alert would have realised in a second that a British army patrol does not wear balaclavas pulled down over their faces. He would have realised immediately it was trap, put his foot hard down and swerved around the men and got out of danger, just as he had in the old days.

But instead, caught by surprise he stopped and the hooded men quickly opened the door of the car and dragged him out. Then he was being frog marched away and the car was being driven off the road and down a track by one of the gang. His hands are being cuffed up hard behind his back, there is a lot of shouting, a lot of effing and blinding.

Then a hood is thrust over his head and he is pitched face forward on to the straw in a barn. At the same time he can hear the car being backed up to the rear of the building.

How long was he forced to lie like that? Certainly not more than five minutes. These men were experts. They had the bomb waiting, they knew what they were doing.

As he lay there he thought of my mother, he thought of Alison and he thought of me. He knew it was quite likely that he would get a bullet in the head. He had known several people who had ended up that way.

When the bomb had been loaded up the door to the barn was reopened, the hood was removed, the handcuffs were taken off and he was put back in the driving seat of the car.

Then one of the hooded men was leaning over him, he could smell the beer on his breath.

He was telling him that there was a one hundred and fifty pound bomb in the back of the car and he had to drive it into the centre of Randalstown where it was timed to go off. They would be following behind him with guns loaded to make sure he did as he was told.

Then he leaned forward offering a few crude epithets before adding, so the Bluffer said, the name of the person who wanted him to go up with the bomb. But the Bluffer, right up until his dying day, never let on who that was.

The Bluffer is later praised for the coolness of his actions. He drives right through the middle of Randalstown shouting out to a policeman that he has been hijacked and that he has a bomb in the car that could kill them all. He is going to make for open country the other side. A lesser man would have abandoned the car in the town. When he is clear of the town he stops and jumps out and runs for his life and thirty seconds later the car explodes with a great whoosh sending earth and stones flying into the air and leaving a bloody great hole beneath it.

The Bluffer had plenty of time to think after that. The same story had repeated itself. As with the factory in Wales he had become reckless, he had over reached himself. There had been that strange evening when the vote had been taken to declare independence for Northern Ireland. There had been the gimlet eyed republicans at the magazine in Dublin. He had also carried money across borders for Edward. Then there were the articles he and Mac had been planning to write. He thought of the long list of enemies he had made and of the people who wanted him blown up along with the citizens of Randalstown. It was time to pull in his horns.

So the Bluffer retired from all those sort of operations. He saw Mac only occasionally and it was a while before he visited Les Valettes again. He mowed his grass and invited the Anglo Irish set to drinks parties and was in turn invited back by them.

But both of them were so shaken by what had happened that they considered leaving Ireland. They looked at houses in the Wye Valley but then said that everything had changed in England, and so they stayed in Ireland. The photographs show the Bluffer's hair has gone from silver to white and the face is perhaps a little more thoughtful. For a long time, until the troubles in Ireland were over, the Bluffer never mentioned the incident with the bomb.

For a time in Ireland the Bluffer had operated a fish farm, but that is not part of this narrative except in the respect that one day, several months before the bomb incident, when he was opening the post he found a letter from Eddie Gallagher addressed from Portlaoise Prison. At the time Eddie Gallagher was one of the most notorious of the IRA gang leaders. For a period, along with English heiress Rose Dugdale, he had run rings round the authorities. There were bombings, kidnappings and thefts of art works before they were caught. Eddie Gallagher had certainly been headline news.

But now, so the letter read, he wanted to set up as a fish farmer when he was eventually released from prison. He had read in a newspaper article that the Bluffer had started a fish farm in County Donegal and he was looking for advice.

In the same way that the Bluffer was the first person to use a microwave oven in a hotel in Mid Wales, he was also the first person to keep trout in the sea in Mulroy Bay, but that is not part of this story.

After getting the first letter the Bluffer entered into a considerable correspondence with Eddie Gallagher and they discussed different aspects of fish farming.

But after the incident with the bomb and worrying that there could have been a connection with Eddie Gallagher, he wound up that correspondence.

# 35

Those last seven years, after the operation, were good years for us.

To begin with, in our optimism, we thought we had reversed the trend, perhaps even found some sort of a cure.

Over the years Supin had gone from stick to frame to wheelchair. After the operation she was back to just a stick. She could even drive the car again. She was also taking less Sinemet so she was calmer and less impulsive.

The proceeds from the robbery had paid for our little house in Cornwall so our money worries, which had dogged us since the closure of the restaurant, were behind us. As the Bluffer might have said, in his elegant way, 'Family finances were restored.'

But over those years she did slowly weaken again, although the twitching and jerking never returned.

We stopped going to the casino but instead we went to the bingo. It was really just for Supin to get out. The other people there must have thought we were an odd couple. But we didn't care. That was a time when we were happy together.

We had our routine. I would get her settled - tablets, water, pens, bingo cards, tea, something to nibble on, perhaps a sandwich or a plate of chips - then I would find a quiet corner where I could read a book or just watch the players. On occasion I would bring along a notebook and sketch out some ideas. I thought I might write a novel. I can see now, though I wasn't aware of it at the time, that really I was making preparations for this memoir.

They were kind people at the bingo and they always kept an eye on her if I went out for any reason.

One thing that should be said about our visits to the bingo was that whatever Supin's physical state her brain still functioned well.

She could easily work two bingo cards at a time - the quickest players could manage three. But her pen still moved over the numbers with a speed most of us would be unable to match.

We didn't go to the bingo because we needed the money. We could afford anything we wanted then. But if she had a win she would always get me to stop at a chip shop before we caught the ferry over to Torpoint. She would take the money out of her purse and I would go in and buy fish and chips and she would eat them as we drove home.

We made other trips out but a lot of the time we were content to stay quietly at home. She talked about setting up our temple, discussing it with Phra Maha Laow on the phone.

When the weather was good I would help her out into the garden and she would busy herself with weeding or pruning, but at other moments she would just sit quietly looking around.

But there was one clue that I missed completely.

In summer our little wooden house was idyllic but in winter, when the weather was bad, it could feel remote.

So now on occasion when we went into Plymouth we would sometimes spend an hour driving along quiet streets looking at houses, in case we needed to move again.

We didn't go to estate agents. We were just looking. We would drive along a street and then park and if Supin was feeling well enough she would get out of the car and look around and point out the sort of house she liked.

Of course when I look back now I can see that what she was actually doing was scouting for me, showing me the sort of places where we could set up our temple when she was gone.

When some months after her death I did walk up the path to one of the houses we had looked at I knew straightway.

I stood in the living room, looked around the bedroom, peered through the kitchen window to the little back garden and then said to the letting agent:

' This is it. This is the place Supin wanted us to take.'

Such is the strange way the world works.

## 36

Toward the end Supin became quite confused.

I should have been more aware of what was happening but the decline was so gradual that we adapted to it without realising how serious it had become.

She began to take her tablets in the wrong order or she could even forget to take them at all. She could leave dishes burning on the stove so that the smoke alarm went off. Her sleep pattern became chaotic and her balance was so bad she was always liable to fall.

Then one night, we had been out all afternoon and she was tired, she fell out of bed.

I had been sitting in the kitchen, thinking how long we could continue in this way, when I heard the thump.

As I struggled to get her back into bed, she was fighting to get her breath and her body had gone rigid, I looked around the room.

Drawers and cupboards were open. Clothes were strewn everywhere. Packets of tablets were open on the table.

The following day I took her in to see our doctor at the surgery in Cawsand. She was using a wheelchair again then. There were just the three of us.

I explained to the doctor what was happening. He looked at me very seriously and then at Supin and then said we could not continue like this. After that he picked up the phone and booked a week's rest at a nursing home for Supin.

So that was another turning point. First and as it turned out last time in a nursing home.

So now we have just left the surgery in Cawsand.

Everything is arranged. Tomorrow she will go into the nursing home for the week. We must have had the last appointment of the day because the light is starting to fade.

As we drive back along the cliff road, I roll the window down to smell the sea. Then I look across to see that Supin's head is back and her eyes are closed. But then her mobile rings and her eyes jerk open and she leans forward and scrabbles in her bag to find and answer it.

Her good friend Chompu wants us go into town to discuss some temple related business.

Suddenly her eyes are wide open, she is talking and concentrating.

'You are exhausted Supin,' I say as she clicks the phone off. 'We need to go home.' But she sets her face, I know that stubborn look, and says nothing.

So on we drive, past the house, down to the river at Torpoint and over into Plymouth. An hour after leaving the surgery we are rolling up to Chompu's house.

There we carried her inside and installed her on a sofa. Food was brought in. There was laughter and shouting. People were telling jokes. The meeting, I forget the detail, was conducted while we ate. Then someone said why don't we have a game of cards and so as the cards were slapped down, we were well past midnight at this point, I heard once again that low rumbling voice and that deep familiar laugh.

A week later, in the nursing home, she was dead.

***

The morning after Supin died, in contrast to our normal blowy cliff top weather the day was still. I went down the steep cliff path and walked along the beach. My life was in a state of suspension such as can only be experienced with something as definitive as a death. As I walked I also knew, with an absolute certainty, that her spirit was ascending upwards toward the heavens. I knew also of course that my life would never be the same again.

***

A week later Phra Maha Laow came down from Kings Bromley with three other monks to conduct the funeral service.

We had private prayers in the house then we went to the crematorium which quickly filled up so that late comers had to stand outside.

When we brought the coffin in we placed a picture of Supin on it. It was one that been taken a long time ago, when she was seventeen years old, that had been enlarged and framed.

She looked extraordinary beautiful and delicate.

(This is really the story of Supin, the Bluffer and myself and how we all got on. We had our own family. Three beautiful kids who were all at the funeral. But this is not a story about them. They still have their lives in front of them).

It was a month after the funeral that Phra Maha Laow called a meeting and made a gracious little speech telling his audience that Supin, whom he had known for twenty years, had confided to him before she died that she would like to see set up a small temple for the Thai and Buddhist people of Plymouth and Cornwall.

He then passed the microphone over to me and I expanded on this theme, telling people about Supin and how she had put up with that bloody Parkinson's disease for all those years and how she had written the story of her life.

After that they made me president of the fund raising committee, but it was our treasurer Michael Kinghorn from St Austell and Chompu Sharpe, our chief fundraiser, who did all the work. I was only on the sidelines.

I stayed in my little house on the Cornish cliff top for a couple of weeks. But then when I felt the ghosts of the past closing in on me I packed a bag and left again.

## 37

Now we are assembled once more.

It is a lovely sunny day in the middle of April, just over two years after the death of Supin. Enough funds have been raised. Our temple is established in a small house on a quiet street in Plymouth. Our Thai monk, sent down from Kings Bromley by Phra Maha Laow, is in residence. The front room is the prayer room and on a low table sits a golden image of the Buddha.

I whittled down the choice of photographs to four.

There was the picture I took when we were at Hilltop in Ireland where we lived before we got married. She is in front of the house in the early morning.

Then there is the portrait we placed on top of the coffin in the crematorium.

There are two other pictures. In one she has had the big win at the casino and is handing out money to the Bangkok street children in a very regal manner.

In the final one she is a teenager in Thailand. She is in a group, there are four of them, in an open top car. She is waving and wearing a sort of sailor's hat.

In the end I didn't choose any of those. Instead I chose one I had taken two years before. She is wearing a turquoise blouse and her mouth is slightly open as if she is speaking. There is a smile on her face. To me it is a picture that combines beauty and wisdom.

I spend some time over the wording. In the end I settled for her name and her dates and the words In Loving Memory.

I chose an afternoon when all the hullabaloo of the official opening of the temple was over, when Phra Maha Laow was back in Kings Bromley, and a routine had been established.

There are always people coming and going, bringing flowers and food. They come to talk to our monk and to say their prayers. It is also a social point where people meet up to chat and gossip.

I pick up the photograph from the framers and drive out to the temple.

The light is not bright. In fact the afternoon is muted. But the daffodils are out and the blossom will be with us soon. Supin used to love the blossom.

The monk has finished his lunch and is talking on the phone. An English woman who I have never seen before and a Thai woman I know by sight are in the little kitchen washing the dishes.

In the living room the gold Buddha image catches a little of the pale sunshine. There is a rich cream carpet on the floor. A gust of wind outside is strong enough to move the leaves on the trees. There is a chance of rain later. The monk puts away his phone and smiles at me. He knows why I am here.

He takes the picture looks at it and smiles again. He says she will be happy here. Then he places the picture among two bunches of flowers next to one of the Buddhas. So that is how, with my duty done, custody of Supin's memory passes over.

# 38

There were times when I find myself confusing the detail of the Bluffer's 90th birthday party and the day of his funeral two years later.

The birthday party was in April. The sun shone, there was a light breeze and we were all in a happy mood.

Even at that age the Bluffer was still aware of everything that was happening around him. He debriefed the postman and the cleaning lady and the other people who visited and soon had the details of all their lives. He also took up Bridge again. This was a game he had learned in the war when he was lying up in a cave on occupied Crete with one of his irregular units.

The set up is elaborate. An ancient table is erected, chairs are unfolded, the nap is brushed. For tea there is a cloth and the best china from the sideboard. There is also a good sherry. We had a retired general but he dropped out and now there are three ladies and the Bluffer, which suits him fine. He will flatter and charm but will give no quarter when it comes to the game. When they have finished and have eaten cake and sandwiches, provided by the ladies, they relax and chat and replay the hands together. They are all good friends.

The funeral, two years later, was in May. A cold wind cut through us and the grey sky threatened rain all day. But the locations were identical and with the exception of Supin the cast for both events was pretty much the same. Supin had been present for the birthday, the group photograph shows her in the front in her wheelchair, but she had gone on by the time of the funeral.

Prior to the birthday the Bluffer had done a two month spell in hospital in Derry. He was first at Altnagelvin and then at the Waterside. He had smashed up his hip. I have often wondered what happened. He had gone out without a torch, at five o'clock on a cold winter's evening when it was already dark and starting to rain, to pick leeks from his vegetable garden for his supper. Did he think he was invincible? He had slipped and fallen and lain there in the mud for twenty minutes shivering before someone found him. When he came out of the hospital they found that his eyes had deteriorated, so they stopped him driving as well.

But lying in his hospital bed he had time to work on his speech for the party. He told me when I went to visit him that his only regret was that neither my mother nor my sister Alison could be present.

They had sold Ballyarr and moved to Northern Ireland to be near Alison when my mother became ill. My mother has been dead ten years now and Alison four.

There was the big leather backed chair which we took out onto the gravel at the front of the house. We placed it carefully, so the sun wasn't in his eyes. Then we gathered around in a semi circle. There were about fifty of us, family and friends, and he spoke for twenty minutes without notes, in a clear strong voice, outlining the various passages of his life.

Then a small plane began to circle above the house. He had just wound up the speech and we had all applauded. Then we watched as the side door opened and the pilot gave the plane a little shrug and shot out into the light a paratrooper who sailed gracefully to the ground in front of us. Then he took off his harness, set his red beret correctly, stepped forward, cracked a smart salute and handed the Bluffer a scroll.

The Bluffer then opened scroll and read out in a clear voice:

'The Parachute Regiment and Airborne Forces.

To Major Ian Smith, MC and bar.

To mark the occasion of your 90th birthday.

Happy Landings.'

It was signed at the bottom, in person, by the Colonel in Chief of the Parachute Regiment.

This was our birthday present to him.

When the Bluffer had returned the paratrooper's salute, slightly lazily I thought, I had seen a tear forming at the corner of his eye. We recorded this event in pictures for the family album but the photographer from the local paper who we asked to attend did not print the image because the activities of the Parachute Regiment are still a sensitive issue in Northern Ireland even today.

While in hospital the Bluffer had given great thought to his lunch party. He even allowed us to hire a small band which played in the corner. Some people danced afterwards and the Bluffer said that was a good idea. The Bluffer invited the three ladies from his bridge circle to join him at the top table, they were all in their nineties also, and he charmed each of them individually. He had the table raised a little, so that it was in the form of a dais, so he could look down on us. The only sadness was that neither Alison nor my mother were present at this event.

On the day of the funeral he was laid out in his coffin in another room in the house. The rector, dressed in black with a red sash, said prayers and then we carried the coffin, high on our shoulders, outside into the cold day.

A week before I had stood at the top of the stairs. I had looked down at the back of his head, he was watching television, and thought it can't be too long now. Soon you are going to migrate to the other side and be with the others and all we will have left is pictures and memories.

(Incidentally, many months after the death and the funeral, and long after the obituary had appeared in the Daily Telegraph, there was a strange coda to Counterpart, the book he wrote. It was a thirty second clip on YouTube. A camera panned across a beach in Scotland and showed thousands of dead fish. Environmental experts said it was pollution, but when I checked and saw that the site was only a few miles from where we had dumped Counterpart, I knew otherwise).

The evening the Bluffer died we had watched the news on television and then I had helped him along the passage to his bedroom. Then he was in the bathroom. I was sitting on the bed. I was going to help him with his shoes.

I watch him as he comes slowly into the bedroom. He is half bent over and leaning on his stick. His great pachyderm eyes are looking directly at me.

Then he sits down on the bed beside me, utters some last words I am not going to repeat and keels over and dies.

Within minutes, or so it seems, the bedroom is full of paramedics and they are bumping him down onto the floor and falling on him and massaging his heart and shocking him until the sweat is running down their faces.

Then a woman comes out who says she is a doctor. It is the middle of the night now. She is Russian and her English is limited. She officially pronounces him dead. As she stands there I wonder what the Bluffer would have said if he could have addressed her. Would he have told her in Russian, perhaps slightly rusty now, that he was proud never to have sent any of those defectors home? No one of us can know that now. I sat up with him the rest of the night.

After the service we took him to the crematorium and that was the end of that. But death isn't a big thing. It happens to us all. The point is to live.

# 39

A memoir, even a short one like this, is not easy to write.

I edited Supin's story and I also wrote the first draft of Ian's obituary that went into the Daily Telegraph. This was taken from a private memoir Ian had written called The Happy Amateur. The obituary was then fleshed out by a professional military historian.

As I wrote as I was confronted by the problem all memoirists have to deal with - which passages of a life to select and which to leave out.

I also became aware that both their stories could have been written in a dozen different ways. All would have produced a different story but all would have been equally true.

So I hope you will forgive me for producing yet another version of your lives.

While you may be surprised by some of the liberties I have taken I hope you will agree that I have stayed faithful to the spirit of who you both were.

# APPENDIX ONE

An extract from the memoir of Supin Smith ( nee Nakornwong ) first published in the Thai Sarn magazine.

## DREAM, HOPE, OBSTACLES AND SUCCESS

Supin Nakornwong grew up in Baan Na District, Nakhon Nayok Province. She began to experience life's difficulties when she was six years old. She was brought to Bangkok by one lady who had travelled to Baan Na to undertake her business in the wood trade. The lady met Supin's mother who was at the time working at the sawmill. The lady made enquiries and saw that Supin's mother was a hard working woman and she realised that she did everything, sawing wood, carrying timber, working on the farm and in the paddy field. Supin's mother had to work hard in order to support her family (Supin's father had died when she was four years old). The lady felt compassion and wanted to relieve Supin's family burden by adopting Supin.

So the lady took Supin to stay at her house in the Sukhumvit area of the city as a friend of her own daughter. As a result Supin's life was completely changed from the country girl who spent each day running around the fields to the life of a civilised upper class family in Bangkok.

***

(Supin stayed with this family for twenty eight years before moving out and marrying and working at first in a beauty salon and then in a golf equipment shop).

***

'But in 1972 (Supin writes) I decided to separate from my husband and to raise my two daughters alone. I did all kinds of hard work but be it easy or hard I did not mind. I made sausages and sold them. I sewed clothes and dresses for babies but the income was not sufficient because I had to look after my two daughters and my daughters and I sometimes went hungry.

Then one afternoon I was waiting for a bus when I noticed Rorie trying to bargain the fair with the taxi driver. He had only fourteen Baht when the fare was fifteen Baht. So hearing the taxi driver scolding Rorie saying: 'Farang you do not even have one Baht,' I felt compassion and gave the one Baht to the taxi driver.

At the same time Rorie, who was foreign editor of the Bangkok Nation Review, was looking for a place to stay so the following day he came round to the house where I was living with my daughters to return the money. I was cooking dinner at the time so I asked him to join us and shortly after he took a spare room in our house.'

( Rorie and Supin then move to Ireland where they get married. They then go to England).

While we ran the Thai Coffee House restaurant in Plymouth I also had an additional job. I taught Thai food cooking at Eggbuckland College twice a week for almost year. I was proud that I was able to teach Thai cooking and to make some contribution to people becoming more aware of Thailand. I had many different people studying with me including lawyers and television personalities.

The first indication that something was wrong was that my feet felt numb and it was becoming more difficult to control my arms and feet. I felt tired and I had no strength. At first neither the GP nor the local hospital could diagnose what was the disease was.

But then after a series of test the doctor said: ' Your disease is incurable, you have Parkinson's disease.'

I could not help myself. The restaurant had to be sold and I waited for the date of the operation.

During that time I could not walk. Rorie had to carry me on his shoulders all the time. It was very painful, when I tried to catch something it just dropped out of my hand I just sat still and became distressed and upset.

Sometimes I could not breathe. I was uncomfortable, trembling, my body seem to be frozen. I could not move I was always tired.

Eventually after Rorie made a special request and our doctor showed great compassion the date of the operation arrived. It was to be performed by the leading British surgeon Mr Steven Gill at Frenchay Hospital in Bristol.

What keeps my life going to day is mindfulness and never giving up.

In the past I could not accept this. I was confused frustrated stressed.

Today I take less medicine and control and calm my mind more through meditation chanting and applying Buddhist teaching. I chant every chapter and extend loving kindness, it helps calm my mind a lot. I extend loving kindness to everyone every day.

Today I am very happy with my life. The Parkinson's disease will always be with me but it is not as terrible as it was before. I meditate every day, I can drive like a normal person. I drive my car to wherever I want to go. When I want to see friends I just jump in the car and drive straightaway. Now Rorie and I have moved to live in Cornwall. We are just by the sea. I am happy with nature because I am growing old so I need to live peacefully in my small house hear the sea growing vegetables and flowers like a normal old person.

I would like to say something to those people who think of giving up. Think afresh, think that you still have hope. We need to have the self confidence that we are capable of achieving what we aim for. Even if it may be a bit late, never give up. Look at my life. I used to think of giving up, but I gave myself moral support. I stand up and move on with my life. One other thing that I am very proud of is that all my three daughters completed their studies and received their university degrees.

Sometimes it is hard to be born a human being. But there are so many things in the world waiting for us. A long time ago I had a dream of flying in an airplane and living abroad and my wish has come true. I think life has a lot of miracles and I would like to remind you that our lives have been through thousands of difficulties. I do not want people to end up in despair. Living abroad we need to be strong all the time.

Look at me as an example, thought I still have this disease I still do not give up.'

# APPENDIX TWO

Daily Telegraph obituary.
May 18th 2012

Major Ian Smith, who has died aged 92, won two Military Crosses while serving with the Commandos, the Special Operations Executive and the Special Boat Squadron.

***

In April 1944 a bombing raid on coastal defences near Deauville was reported to have set off a series of flashes on the beach. Four reconnaissance operations, code-named Tarbrush, were therefore mounted at short notice to examine mines and obstacles in the region — though not on the D-Day beaches themselves for fear of attracting attention to them.

In May, Smith was called to Combined Operations HQ for a top-level briefing. His orders were to find out whether explosive devices had been attached to the tops of stakes that the Germans had erected on the beaches. If they had, when detonated they might buckle the doors of the landing craft and the soldiers trapped inside would be sitting targets.

On the moonless night of May 16, Smith, at the head of a small detachment of 10 (Inter-Allied) Commando, embarked from Dover in an MTB. Their engine-powered dory was dropped a mile offshore and they landed by dinghy east of Calais.

Armed with a Sten gun and accompanied by a sapper, Smith crawled up the beach.

The smell of cigarette smoke alerted them to the presence of a sentry. Then they heard German spoken. The guard was being changed.

The sapper groped his way up one of the stakes and found an anti-tank Teller mine nailed to the top. Having decided not to remove it because the sentry would be sure to hear the noise, they returned to their dory, slid over the side and paddled until they were far enough from the beach to start the engine.

They transmitted their call sign by "S" phone, an early "walkie-talkie", but received no answer from the MTB. A ship approached them and, turning on its searchlight, scanned the sea. The Germans permitted no fishing at night, and Smith feared that it was one of their armed naval trawlers.

They flattened themselves on the bottom of the dory. The vessel sailed past only a few yards away, and Smith said afterwards: "How it did not see us, I shall never know." Some minutes later it turned about and, directed by its radar or shore radar, loosed off some heavy gunfire in their direction.

Just as it was getting very close there came a sudden ringing of bells and shouted orders and, having apparently become stuck on a sand bank, it stopped. Smith and his party eventually found the MTB, which had moved out to sea to avoid the trawler. Smith celebrated the success of the operation in a series of Dover hostelries and became so inebriated that his batman had to take him home in a wheelbarrow. He was awarded a Bar to an earlier MC.

Ian Christopher Downs Smith was born at Keynsham, near Bristol, on April 22 1920 and educated at Wycliffe College. In 1939, as a cadet at Sandhurst, he was one of a party taken to Aldershot to see an armoured division. Interspersed with a few tanks were soldiers holding up green flags. When asked what they were doing, they sprang to attention and replied: "I am a Mark II Tank, sir."

Smith played rugby for Sandhurst, Harlequins and the Army. Shortly after being commissioned into the Royal

Army Service Corps, he volunteered to join No 2 Commando, the precursor of the Parachute Regiment, later termed the 1st Battalion Parachute Regiment, and trained at Ringway, where he and his comrades were reviewed by a disgruntled Churchill who was counting on getting many more volunteers.

In 1940 he moved to Lochailort in Scotland, where he was trained in unarmed combat, pistol shooting and explosives. A spell at Achnacarry as an instructor in fieldcraft was followed by a posting to No 12 Commando. He then moved to Shetland to work with a Norwegian motor torpedo boat flotilla and was based at Sullom Voe.

On reconnaissance missions to spy on the shipping in Norwegian territorial waters, they set off from Lerwick and hoisted the German naval ensign as they approached the coast. After creeping down a narrow channel in the cliff face, they docked, camouflaging the boat during the hours of daylight.

Smith was then ordered to the Isle of Wight, where he became part of Fynn Force, based at Freshwater Bay. In September 1943 he was part of a small unit that was landed between Dieppe and Le Havre to report on the enemy's coastal defences.

Forbidden to use radio signals, they were provided with carrier pigeons to send back their information. But when they released one of the birds, it was promptly killed by a peregrine falcon; a second pigeon met the same fate.

In December that year Smith and a small group embarked at Newhaven and crossed the Channel in an MTB on a reconnaissance mission. They landed on the north coast of France near Criel-Sur-Mer and had a difficult climb to the top of the cliff. Smith returned with valuable information on the German defences, but on the way back to the MTB they were almost cut off by a fast-moving enemy convoy, and Smith needed all his navigating skills to elude it. He was awarded his first MC, the citation stating that he had led eight previous operations of a similar type.

Shortly before D-Day, Smith was recruited by the SOE and flew to Italy. In Bari, he was told that he was to be dropped into Yugoslavia to join Brigadier Fitzroy Maclean's mission and serve as British Liaison Officer with the 5th Partisan Corps in Bosnia.

As he parachuted down, he heard a voice call out: "In a hurry, are you sir?" It was Corporal Nash, his signaller and bodyguard, whom he had overtaken because he was much heavier. Sharing a nomadic life in the mountains with the partisans, he was constantly on the move dodging enemy patrols as he arranged for supply drops of food and arms, called in air support when an attack was launched against the Germans and helped evacuate those who were badly wounded or downed American airmen.

On the way back to Bari in a Tank Landing Ship, Smith was enjoying a shot of Navy rum with the boatswain when the steel walls of the cabin bent inwards as if they had received a blow from a gigantic hammer. A Liberty ship, loaded with thousands of tons of high explosives had blown up, causing devastation in the Italian port and great loss of life.

Smith was then attached to the Special Boat Squadron and commanded a small force in Crete. Living in a large cave and based in the east of the island, their task was to watch the remnants of the German and Italian occupiers and report back to their base.

A spell on the Greek mainland, followed by a raid on the Dalmatian island of Cres, brought Smith's active service to an end. When the war ended, he was promoted to major, and after commanding an RASC unit at Bicester he went up to Jesus College, Cambridge, to learn Russian.

He was then posted to Minden in western Germany, where he interrogated deserters from the Soviet forces who were suspected of being agents posing as refugees. In 1947 he joined the family textile business at Stockport, Cheshire, eventually moving with the firm to Wales. He then managed a hotel for five years. In the 1970s he moved to Co Donegal, where he started a fish farm.

In August 1974 Smith was driving a car near Randalstown, Northern Ireland, when he was forced to stop by three armed masked men. They tied him up, put a bomb in his car and then ordered him to drive into town and park by an electrical shop. They told him that they would follow him and shoot him if he did not do what they wanted and that the bomb was timed to go off in 20 minutes. At the shop there were several members of the RUC, who told him not to stop but to drive out of town. He found a field, left the car and ran for his life. The bomb exploded on time.

Smith spent the last decade of his life in Northern Ireland. Watching rugby matches was his favourite recreation.

Ian Smith married, in 1944, Margaret (Peggy) Cropper. She predeceased him. A daughter Alison also predeceased him. He is survived by their son Rorie.